ARSÈNE LUPIN VERSUS HERLOCK SHOLMES

MAURICE LEBLANC

Classic Editions

Arsène Lupin versus Herlock Sholmes
By Maurice Leblanc
Complete and Unabridged

ISBN NO. 978-1-80445-001-7

Classic Editions

This edition published by
Fox Eye Publishing Ltd.
Vulcan House Business Centre
Vulcan Road, Leicester, LE5 3EF
United Kingdom

This edition is published in 2022

Cover Design by Haitenlo Semy
Cover images © Shutterstock

In association with
Wilco Publishing House
Mumbai, India.

© *Wilco* Publishing House 2021

Printed and bound in India

About the Author

MAURICE LEBLANC

Born on 11 December 1864 in Rouen, France, Maurice-Marie-Émile Leblanc, better known Maurice Leblanc, was a French journalist and author. He was the second child of Emile Leblanc, who was of Italian ancestry, and Blance Brohy. He was educated at the Lycée Pierre Corneille in Rouen and also studied in Germany and Italy before eventually dropping out of law school to pursue his interest in writing.

Leblanc began his career as a journalist, until he was asked to write a short story filler for the French periodical Je sais tout to outshine the charm of Sherlock Holmes. Thus was born the character of Arsene Lupin in "L'Arrestation d'Arsène Lupin" ("The Arrest of Arsène Lupin") — the gentleman thief and detective — as France's answer to all things charming, witty, clever and a fine example of upmanship, all set to dethrone the popularity of Arthur Conan Doyles' most-loved character.

While Lupin has become a household name today due to the highly successful Netflix series based on his exploits, many of Leblanc's stories were adapted into successful theatre productions and films as early as the 1930's.

Lupin is created as an interesting character — witty, brilliant, generous, but not completely without shades of grey. The less fortunate often profit from his large heart. The rich and powerful, and the detective Mainard, who tries to spoil his fun, however, must beware. They are the target of Lupin's adventures and mischief. The elaborate plots, the twists in the tales, his ability to wriggle out of the most impossible situations have enraptured readers down the decades.

Leblanc introduced Sherlock Holmes into the Lupin series but was forced to rename the character Herlock Sholmes in the second book after Sir Arthur Conan Doyle complained about the use of his detective. The U.S. versions went a step further and replaced 'Herlock Sholmes' with 'Holmlock Shears'.

In 1930, after the death of Arthur Conan Doyle, Maurice Leblanc wrote a warm homage: A propos de Conan Doyle (About Conan Doyle) for the French magazine Les Annales Politiques et Littéraires on 1 August 1930.

Although Leblanc created other characters over the years, including the moderately popular private eye Jim Barnett, he always returned to his most successful character — Lupin. Leblanc once said 'Lupin follows me everywhere. He is not my shadow. I am his shadow.'

There are twenty volumes in the Arsène Lupin series written by Leblanc himself, plus five authorized sequels written by mystery writers Boileau and Narcejac.

Leblanc also penned two science fiction novels: Les Trois Yeux in 1919 and Le Formidable Evènement in 1920.

Leblanc was awarded the French Legion of Honour for his services to literature in 1912.

To escape the German occupation, he fled to Paris along with his family where he spent his remaining years until he died on 6 November 1941 and was buried in the Montparnasse Cemetery.

CONTENTS

CONTENTS

Chapter 1

LOTTERY TICKET NO. 514

ON the eighth day of last December, Mon. Gerbois, professor of mathematics at the College of Versailles, while rummaging in an old curiosity-shop, unearthed a small mahogany writing-desk which pleased him very much on account of the multiplicity of its drawers.

"Just the thing for Suzanne's birthday present," thought he. And as he always tried to furnish some simple pleasures for his daughter, consistent with his modest income, he enquired the price, and, after some keen bargaining, purchased it for sixty-five francs. As he was giving his address to the shopkeeper, a young man, dressed with elegance and taste, who had been exploring the stock of antiques, caught sight of the writing-desk, and immediately enquired its price.

"It is sold," replied the shopkeeper.

"Ah! To this gentleman, I presume?"

Monsieur Gerbois bowed, and left the store, quite proud to be the possessor of an article which had attracted the attention of a gentleman of quality. But he had not taken a dozen steps in the street, when he was overtaken by the young man who, hat in hand and in a tone of perfect courtesy, thus addressed him:

"I beg your pardon, monsieur; I am going to ask you a question that you may deem impertinent. It is this: Did you have any special object in view when you bought that writing-desk?"

"No, I came across it by chance and it struck my fancy."

"But you do not care for it particularly?"

"Oh! I shall keep it—that is all."

"Because it is an antique, perhaps?"

"No; because it is convenient," declared Mon. Gerbois.

"In that case, you would consent to exchange it for another desk that would be quite as convenient and in better condition?"

"Oh! This one is in good condition, and I see no object in making an exchange."

"But—"

Mon. Gerbois is a man of irritable disposition and hasty temper. So he replied, testily:

"I beg of you, monsieur, do not insist."

But the young man firmly held his ground.

"I don't know how much you paid for it, monsieur, but I offer you double."

"No."

"Three times the amount."

"Oh! That will do," exclaimed the professor, impatiently; "I don't wish to sell it."

The young man stared at him for a moment in a manner that Mon. Gerbois would not readily forget, then turned and walked rapidly away.

An hour later, the desk was delivered at the professor's house on the Viroflay road. He called his daughter, and said:

"Here is something for you, Suzanne, provided you like it."

Suzanne was a pretty girl, with a gay and affectionate nature. She threw her arms around her father's neck and kissed him rapturously. To her, the desk had all the semblance of a royal gift. That evening, assisted by Hortense, the servant, she placed the desk in her room; then she dusted it, cleaned the drawers and pigeon-holes, and carefully arranged within it her papers, writing material, correspondence, a collection of post-cards, and some souvenirs of her cousin Philippe that she kept in secret.

Next morning, at half past seven, Mon. Gerbois went to the college. At ten o'clock, in pursuance of her usual custom, Suzanne went to meet him, and it was a great pleasure for him to see her slender figure and childish smile waiting for him at the college gate. They returned home together.

"And your writing desk—how is it this morning?"

"Marvellous! Hortense and I have polished the brass mountings until they look like gold."

"So you are pleased with it?"

"Pleased with it! Why, I don't see how I managed to get on without it for such a long time."

As they were walking up the pathway to the house, Mon. Gerbois said:

"Shall we go and take a look at it before breakfast?"

"Oh! Yes, that's a splendid idea!"

She ascended the stairs ahead of her father, but, on arriving at the door of her room, she uttered a cry of surprise and dismay.

"What's the matter?" stammered Mon. Gerbois.

"The writing-desk is gone!"

When the police were called in, they were astonished at the admirable simplicity of the means employed by the thief. During Suzanne's absence, the servant had gone to market, and while the house was thus left unguarded, a drayman, wearing a badge—some of the neighbours saw it—stopped his cart in front of the house and rang twice. Not knowing that Hortense was absent, the neighbours were not suspicious; consequently, the man carried on his work in peace and tranquillity.

Apart from the desk, not a thing in the house had been disturbed. Even Suzanne's purse, which she had left upon the writing-desk, was found upon an adjacent table with its contents untouched. It was obvious that the thief had come with a set purpose, which rendered the crime even more mysterious; because, why did he assume so great a risk for such a trifling object?

The only clue the professor could furnish was the strange incident of the preceding evening. He declared:

"The young man was greatly provoked at my refusal, and I had an idea that he threatened me as he went away."

But the clue was a vague one. The shopkeeper could not throw any light on the affair. He did not know either of the gentlemen. As to the desk itself, he had purchased it for forty francs at an executor's sale at Chevreuse, and believed he had resold it at its fair value. The police investigation disclosed nothing more.

But Mon. Gerbois entertained the idea that he had suffered an enormous loss. There must have been a fortune concealed in a secret drawer, and that was the reason the young man had resorted to crime.

"My poor father, what would we have done with that fortune?" asked Suzanne.

"My child! With such a fortune, you could make a most advantageous marriage."

Suzanne sighed bitterly. Her aspirations soared no higher than her cousin Philippe, who was indeed a most deplorable object. And life, in the little house at Versailles, was not so happy and contented as of yore.

Two months passed away. Then came a succession of startling events, a strange blending of good luck and dire misfortune!

On the first day of February, at half-past five, Mon. Gerbois entered the house, carrying an evening paper, took a seat, put on his spectacles, and commenced to read. As politics did not interest him, he turned to the inside of the paper. Immediately his attention was attracted by an article entitled:

"Third Drawing of the Press Association Lottery.

"No. 514, series 23, draws a million."

The newspaper slipped from his fingers. The walls swam before his eyes, and his heart ceased to beat. He held No. 514, series 23. He had purchased it from a friend, to oblige him, without any thought of success, and behold, it was the lucky number!

Quickly, he took out his memorandum-book. Yes, he was quite right. The No. 514, series 23, was written there, on the inside of the cover. But the ticket?

He rushed to his desk to find the envelope-box in which he had placed the precious ticket; but the box was not there, and it suddenly occurred to him that it had not been there for several weeks. He heard footsteps on the gravel walk leading from the street.

He called:

"Suzanne! Suzanne!"

She was returning from a walk. She entered hastily. He stammered, in a choking voice:

"Suzanne... the box... the box of envelopes?"

"What box?"

"The one I bought at the Louvre... one Saturday... it was at the end of that table."

"Don't you remember, father, we put all those things away together."

"When?"

"The evening... you know... the same evening..."

"But where?... Tell me, quick!... Where?"

"Where? Why, in the writing-desk."

"In the writing-desk that was stolen?"

"Yes."

"Oh, mon Dieu!... In the stolen desk!"

He uttered the last sentence in a low voice, in a sort of stupor. Then he seized her hand, and in a still lower voice, he said:

"It contained a million, my child."

"Ah! father, why didn't you tell me?" she murmured, naively.

"A million!" he repeated. "It contained the ticket that drew the grand prize in the Press Lottery."

The colossal proportions of the disaster overwhelmed them, and for a long time they maintained a silence that they feared to break. At last, Suzanne said:

"But, father, they will pay you just the same."

"How? On what proof?"

"Must you have proof?"

"Of course."

"And you haven't any?"

"It was in the box."

"In the box that has disappeared."

"Yes; and now the thief will get the money."

"Oh! That would be terrible, father. You must prevent it."

For a moment he was silent; then, in an outburst of energy, he leaped up, stamped on the floor, and exclaimed:

"No, no, he shall not have that million; he shall not have it! Why should he have it? Ah! clever as he is, he can do nothing. If he goes to claim the money, they will arrest him. Ah! now, we will see, my fine fellow!"

"What will you do, father?"

"Defend our just rights, whatever happens! And we will succeed. The million francs belong to me, and I intend to have them."

A few minutes later, he sent this telegram:

"Governor Crédit Foncier

"rue Capucines, Paris.

"Am holder of No. 514, series 23. Oppose by all legal means any other claimant.

"GERBOIS."

Almost at the same moment, the Crédit Foncier received the following telegram:

"No. 514, series 23, is in my possession.

"ARSÈNE LUPIN."

Every time I undertake to relate one of the many extraordinary adventures that mark the life of Arsène Lupin, I experience a feeling of embarrassment, as it seems to me that the most commonplace of those adventures is already well known to my readers. In fact, there is not a movement of our "national thief," as he has been so aptly described, that has not been given the widest publicity, not an exploit that has not been studied in all its phases, not an action that has not been discussed with that particularity usually reserved for the recital of heroic deeds.

For instance, who does not know the strange history of "The Blonde Lady," with those curious episodes which were proclaimed by the newspapers with heavy black headlines, as follows: "Lottery Ticket No. 514!" ... "The Crime on the Avenue Henri-Martin!" ... "The Blue Diamond!" ... The interest created by the intervention of the celebrated English detective, Herlock Sholmes! The excitement aroused by the various vicissitudes which marked the struggle between those famous artists! And what a commotion on the boulevards, the day on which the newsboys announced: "Arrest of Arsène Lupin!"

My excuse for repeating these stories at this time is the fact that I produce the key to the enigma. Those adventures have always been enveloped in a certain degree of obscurity, which I now remove. I reproduce old newspaper articles, I relate old-time interviews, I present ancient letters; but I have arranged and classified all that material and reduced it to the exact truth. My collaborators in this work have been Arsène Lupin himself, and also the ineffable Wilson, the friend and confidant of Herlock Sholmes.

Everyone will recall the tremendous burst of laughter which greeted the publication of those two telegrams. The name "Arsène Lupin" was in itself a stimulus to curiosity, a promise of amusement for the gallery. And, in this case, the gallery means the entire world.

An investigation was immediately commenced by the Crédit Foncier, which established these facts: That ticket No. 514, series 23, had been sold by the Versailles branch office of the Lottery to an artillery officer named Bessy, who was afterward killed by a fall from his horse. Sometime before his death, he informed some of his comrades that he had transferred his ticket to a friend.

"And I am that friend," affirmed Mon. Gerbois.

"Prove it," replied the governor of the Crédit Foncier.

"Of course I can prove it. Twenty people can tell you that I was an intimate friend of Monsieur Bessy, and that we frequently met at the Café de la Place-d'Armes. It was there, one day, I purchased the ticket from him for twenty francs—simply as an accommodation to him.

"Have you any witnesses to that transaction?"

"No."

"Well, how do you expect to prove it?"

"By a letter he wrote to me."

"What letter?"

"A letter that was pinned to the ticket."

"Produce it."

"It was stolen at the same time as the ticket."

"Well, you must find it."

It was soon learned that Arsène Lupin had the letter. A short paragraph appeared in the *Echo de France*—which has the honour to be his official organ, and of which, it is said, he is one of the principal shareholders—the paragraph announced that Arsène Lupin had placed in the hands of Monsieur Detinan, his advocate and legal adviser, the letter that Monsieur Bessy had written to him—to him personally.

This announcement provoked an outburst of laughter. Arsène Lupin had engaged a lawyer! Arsène Lupin, conforming to the rules and customs of modern society, had appointed a legal representative in the person of a well-known member of the Parisian bar!

Mon. Detinan had never enjoyed the pleasure of meeting Arsène Lupin—a fact he deeply regretted—but he had actually been retained by that mysterious gentleman and felt greatly honoured by the choice. He was prepared to defend the interests of his client to the best of his ability. He was pleased, even proud, to exhibit the letter of Mon. Bessy, but, although it proved the transfer of the ticket, it did not mention the name of the purchaser. It was simply addressed to "My Dear Friend."

"My Dear Friend! That is I," added Arsène Lupin, in a note attached to Mon. Bessy's letter. "And the best proof of that fact is that I hold the letter."

The swarm of reporters immediately rushed to see Mon. Gerbois, who could only repeat:

"My Dear Friend! that is I... Arsène Lupin stole the letter with the lottery ticket."

"Let him prove it!" retorted Lupin to the reporters.

"He must have done it, because he stole the writing-desk!" exclaimed Mon. Gerbois before the same reporters.

"Let him prove it!" replied Lupin.

Such was the entertaining comedy enacted by the two claimants of ticket No. 514; and the calm demeanour of Arsène Lupin contrasted strangely with the nervous perturbation of poor Mon. Gerbois. The newspapers were filled with the lamentations of that unhappy man. He announced his misfortune with pathetic candour.

"Understand, gentlemen, it was Suzanne's dowry that the rascal stole! Personally, I don't care a straw for it... but for Suzanne! Just think of it, a whole million! Ten times one hundred thousand francs! Ah! I knew very well that the desk contained a treasure!"

It was in vain to tell him that his adversary, when stealing the desk, was unaware that the lottery ticket was in it, and that, in any event, he could not foresee that the ticket would draw the grand prize. He would reply;

"Nonsense! Of course, he knew it... else why would he take the trouble to steal a poor, miserable desk?"

"For some unknown reason; but certainly not for a small scrap of paper which was then worth only twenty francs."

"A million francs! He knew it... he knows everything! Ah! You do not know him—the scoundrel!... He hasn't robbed you of a million francs!"

The controversy would have lasted for a much longer time, but, on the twelfth day, Mon. Gerbois received from Arsène Lupin a letter, marked "confidential", which read as follows:

"Monsieur, the gallery is being amused at our expense. Do you not think it is time for us to be serious? The situation is this: I possess a ticket to which I have no legal right, and you have the legal right to a ticket you do not possess. Neither of us can do anything. You will not relinquish your rights to me; I will not deliver the ticket to you. Now, what is to be done?

"I see only one way out of the difficulty: Let us divide the spoils. A half-million for you; a half-million for me. Is not that a fair division? In my opinion, it is an equitable solution, and an immediate one. I will give you three days' time to consider the proposition. On Thursday morning I shall expect to read in the personal column of the Echo de France a discreet message addressed to *M. Ars. Lup*, expressing in veiled terms your consent to my offer. By so doing you will recover immediate possession of the ticket; then you can collect the money and send me half a million in a manner that I will describe to you later.

"In case of your refusal, I shall resort to other measures to accomplish the same result. But, apart from the very serious annoyances that such obstinacy on your part will cause you, it will cost you twenty-five thousand francs for supplementary expenses.

"Believe me, monsieur, I remain your devoted servant, ARSÈNE LUPIN."

In a fit of exasperation Mon. Gerbois committed the grave mistake of showing that letter and allowing a copy of it to be taken. His indignation overcame his discretion.

"Nothing! He shall have nothing!" he exclaimed, before a crowd of reporters. "To divide my property with him? Never! Let him tear up the ticket if he wishes!"

"Yet five hundred thousand francs is better than nothing."

"That is not the question. It is a question of my just right, and that right I will establish before the courts."

"What! Attack Arsène Lupin? That would be amusing."

"No; but the Crédit Foncier. They must pay me the million francs."

"Without producing the ticket, or, at least, without proving that you bought it?"

"That proof exists, since Arsène Lupin admits that he stole the writing-desk."

"But would the word of Arsène Lupin carry any weight with the court?"

"No matter; I will fight it out."

The gallery shouted with glee; and wagers were freely made upon the result with the odds in favour of Lupin. On the following Thursday the personal column in the *Echo de France* was eagerly perused by the expectant public, but it contained nothing addressed to *M. Ars. Lup.* Mon. Gerbois had not replied to Arsène Lupin's letter. That was the declaration of war.

That evening the newspapers announced the abduction of Mlle. Suzanne Gerbois.

The most entertaining feature in what might be called the Arsène Lupin dramas is the comic attitude displayed by the Parisian police. Arsène Lupin talks, plans, writes, commands, threatens and executes as if the police did not exist. They never figure in his calculations.

And yet the police do their utmost. But what can they do against such a foe—a foe that scorns and ignores them?

Suzanne had left the house at twenty minutes to ten; such was the testimony of the servant. On leaving the college, at five minutes past ten, her father did not find her at the place she was accustomed to wait for him. Consequently, whatever had happened must have occurred during the course of Suzanne's walk from the house to the college. Two neighbours had met her about three hundred yards from the house. A lady had seen, on the avenue, a young girl corresponding to Suzanne's description. No one else had seen her.

Inquiries were made in all directions; the employees of the railways and street-car lines were questioned, but none of them had seen anything of the missing girl. However, at Ville-d'Avray, they found a shopkeeper who had furnished gasoline to an automobile that had come from Paris on the day of the abduction. It was occupied by a blonde woman—extremely blonde, said the witness. An hour later, the automobile again passed through Ville-d'Avray on its way from Versailles to Paris. The shopkeeper declared that the automobile now contained a second woman who was heavily veiled. No doubt, it was Suzanne Gerbois.

The abduction must have taken place in broad daylight, on a frequented street, in the very heart of the town. How? And at what spot? Not a cry was heard; not a suspicious action had been seen. The shopkeeper described the automobile as a royal-blue limousine of twenty-four horse-power made by the firm of Peugeon & Co. Inquiries were then made at the Grand-Garage, managed by Madame Bob-Walthour, who made a specialty of abductions by automobile. It was learned that she had rented a Peugeon limousine on that day to a blonde woman whom she had never seen before nor since.

"Who was the chauffeur?"

"A young man named Ernest, whom I had engaged only the day before. He came well recommended."

"Is he here now?"

"No. He brought back the machine, but I haven't seen him since," said Madame Bob-Walthour.

"Do you know where we can find him?"

"You might see the people who recommended him to me. Here are the names."

Upon inquiry, it was learned that none of these people knew the man called Ernest. The recommendations were forged.

Such was the fate of every clue followed by the police. It ended nowhere. The mystery remained unsolved.

Mon. Gerbois had not the strength or courage to wage such an unequal battle. The disappearance of his daughter crushed him; he capitulated to the enemy. A short announcement in the *Echo de France* proclaimed his unconditional surrender.

Two days later, Mon. Gerbois visited the office of the Crédit Foncier and handed lottery ticket number 514, series 23, to the governor, who exclaimed, with surprise:

"Ah! you have it! He has returned it to you!"

"It was mislaid. That was all," replied Mon. Gerbois.

"But you pretended that it had been stolen."

"At first, I thought it had... but here it is."

"We will require some evidence to establish your right to the ticket."

"Will the letter of the purchaser, Monsieur Bessy, be sufficient!"

"Yes, that will do."

"Here it is," said Mon. Gerbois, producing the letter.

"Very well. Leave these papers with us. The rules of the lottery allow us fifteen days' time to investigate your claim. I will let you know when to call for your money. I presume you desire, as much as I do, that this affair should be closed without further publicity."

"Quite so."

Mon. Gerbois and the governor henceforth maintained a discreet silence. But the secret was revealed in some way, for it was soon commonly known that Arsène Lupin had returned the lottery ticket to Mon. Gerbois. The public received the news with astonishment and admiration. Certainly, he was a bold gamester who thus threw upon the table a trump card of such importance as the precious ticket. But, it was true, he still retained a trump card of equal importance. However, if the young girl should escape? If the hostage held by Arsène Lupin should be rescued?

The police thought they had discovered the weak spot of the enemy, and now redoubled their efforts. Arsène Lupin disarmed by his own act, crushed by the wheels of his own machination, deprived of every sou of the coveted million... public interest now centred in the camp of his adversary.

But it was necessary to find Suzanne. And they did not find her, nor did she escape. Consequently, it must be admitted, Arsène Lupin had won the first hand. But the game was not yet decided. The most difficult point remained. Mlle. Gerbois is in his possession, and he will hold her until he receives five hundred thousand francs. But how and where will such an exchange be made? For that purpose, a meeting must be arranged, and then what will prevent Mon. Gerbois from warning the police and, in that way, effecting the rescue of his daughter and, at the same time, keeping his money? The professor was interviewed, but he was extremely reticent. His answer was:

"I have nothing to say."

"And Mlle. Gerbois?"

"The search is being continued."

"But Arsène Lupin has written to you?"

"No."

"Do you swear to that?"

"No."

"Then it is true. What are his instructions?"

"I have nothing to say."

Then the interviewers attacked Mon. Detinan, and found him equally discreet.

"Monsieur Lupin is my client, and I cannot discuss his affairs," he replied, with an affected air of gravity.

These mysteries served to irritate the gallery. Obviously, some secret negotiations were in progress. Arsène Lupin had arranged and tightened the meshes of his net, while the police maintained a close watch, day and night, over Mon. Gerbois. And the three and only possible dénouements—the arrest, the triumph, or the ridiculous and pitiful abortion—were freely discussed; but the curiosity of the public was only partially satisfied, and it was reserved for these pages to reveal the exact truth of the affair.

On Monday, March 12th, Mon. Gerbois received a notice from the Crédit Foncier. On Wednesday, he took the one o'clock train for Paris. At two o'clock, a thousand bank-notes of one thousand francs each were delivered to him. Whilst he was counting them, one by one, in a state of nervous agitation—that money, which represented Suzanne's ransom—a carriage containing two men stopped at the curb a short distance from the bank. One of the men had grey hair and an unusually shrewd expression which formed a striking contrast to his shabby make-up. It was Detective Ganimard, the relentless enemy of Arsène Lupin. Ganimard said to his companion, Folenfant:

"In five minutes, we will see our clever friend Lupin. Is everything ready?"

"Yes."

"How many men have we?"

"Eight—two of them on bicycles."

"Enough, but not too many. On no account, must Gerbois escape us; if he does, it is all up. He will meet Lupin at the appointed place, give half a million in exchange for the girl, and the game will be over."

"But why doesn't Gerbois work with us? That would be the better way, and he could keep all the money himself."

"Yes, but he is afraid that if he deceives the other, he will not get his daughter."

"What other?"

"Lupin."

Ganimard pronounced the word in a solemn tone, somewhat timidly, as if he were speaking of some supernatural creature whose claws he already felt.

"It is very strange," remarked Folenfant, judiciously, "that we are obliged to protect this gentleman contrary to his own wishes."

"Yes, but Lupin always turns the world upside down," said Ganimard, mournfully.

A moment later, Mon. Gerbois appeared, and started up the street. At the end of the rue des Capucines, he turned into the boulevards, walking slowly, and stopping frequently to gaze at the shop-windows.

"Much too calm, too self-possessed," said Ganimard. "A man with a million in his pocket would not have that air of tranquillity."

"What is he doing?"

"Oh! nothing, evidently... But I have a suspicion that it is Lupin—yes, Lupin!"

At that moment, Mon. Gerbois stopped at a news-stand, purchased a paper, unfolded it and commenced to read it as he walked slowly away. A moment later, he gave a sudden bound into an automobile that was standing at the curb. Apparently, the machine had been waiting for him, as it started away rapidly, turned at the Madeleine and disappeared.

"Nom de nom!" cried Ganimard, "that's one of his old tricks!"

Ganimard hastened after the automobile around the Madeleine. Then, he burst into laughter. At the entrance to the Boulevard Malesherbes, the automobile had stopped and Mon. Gerbois had alighted.

"Quick, Folenfant, the chauffeur! It may be the man Ernest."

Folenfant interviewed the chauffeur. His name was Gaston; he was an employee of the automobile cab company; ten minutes ago, a gentleman had engaged him and told him to wait near the news-stand for another gentleman.

"And the second man—what address did he give?" asked Folenfant.

"No address. 'Boulevard Malesherbes ... avenue de Messine ... double pourboire.' That is all."

But, during this time, Mon. Gerbois had leaped into the first passing carriage.

"To the Concorde station, Metropolitan," he said to the driver.

He left the underground at the Place du Palais-Royal, ran to another carriage and ordered it to go to the Place de la Bourse. Then a second journey by the underground to the Avenue de Villiers, followed by a third carriage drive to number 25 rue Clapeyron.

Number 25 rue Clapeyron is separated from the Boulevard des Batignolles by the house which occupies the angle formed by the two streets. He ascended to the first floor and rang. A gentleman opened the door.

"Does Monsieur Detinan live here?"

"Yes, that is my name. Are you Monsieur Gerbois?"

"Yes."

"I was expecting you. Step in."

As Mon. Gerbois entered the lawyer's office, the clock struck three. He said:

"I am prompt to the minute. Is he here?"

"Not yet."

Mon. Gerbois took a seat, wiped his forehead, looked at his watch as if he did not know the time, and inquired, anxiously:

"Will he come?"

"Well, monsieur," replied the lawyer, "that I do not know, but I am quite as anxious and impatient as you are to find out. If he comes, he will run a great risk, as this house has been closely watched for the last two weeks. They distrust me."

"They suspect me, too. I am not sure whether the detectives lost sight of me or not on my way here."

"But you were—"

"It wouldn't be my fault," cried the professor, quickly. "You cannot reproach me. I promised to obey his orders, and I followed them to the very letter. I drew the money at the time fixed by him, and I came here in the manner directed by him. I have faithfully performed my part of the agreement—let him do his!"

After a short silence, he asked, anxiously:

"He will bring my daughter, won't he?"

"I expect so."

"But... you have seen him?"

"I? No, not yet. He made the appointment by letter, saying both of you would be here, and asking me to dismiss my servants before three o'clock and admit no one while you were here. If I would not consent to that arrangement, I was to notify him by a few words in *the Echo de France*. But I am only too happy to oblige Mon. Lupin, and so I consented."

"Ah! How will this end?" moaned Mon. Gerbois.

He took the bank-notes from his pocket, placed them on the table and divided them into two equal parts. Then the two men sat there in silence. From time to time, Mon. Gerbois would listen. Did someone ring?... His nervousness increased every minute, and Monsieur Detinan also displayed considerable anxiety. At last, the lawyer lost his patience. He rose abruptly, and said:

"He will not come... We shouldn't expect it. It would be folly on his part. He would run too great a risk."

And Mon. Gerbois, despondent, his hands resting on the bank-notes, stammered:

"Oh! Mon Dieu! I hope he will come. I would give the whole of that money to see my daughter again."

The door opened.

"Half of it will be sufficient, Monsieur Gerbois."

These words were spoken by a well-dressed young man who now entered the room and was immediately recognized by Mon. Gerbois as the person who had wished to buy the desk from him at Versailles. He rushed toward him.

"Where is my daughter—my Suzanne?"

Arsène Lupin carefully closed the door, and, while slowly removing his gloves, said to the lawyer:

"My dear maître, I am indebted to you very much for your kindness in consenting to defend my interests. I shall not forget it."

Mon. Detinan murmured:

"But you did not ring. I did not hear the door—"

"Doors and bells are things that should work without being heard. I am here, and that is the important point."

"My daughter! Suzanne! Where is she!" repeated the professor.

"Mon Dieu, monsieur," said Lupin, "what's your hurry? Your daughter will be here in a moment."

Lupin walked to and fro for a minute, then, with the pompous air of an orator, he said:

"Monsieur Gerbois, I congratulate you on the clever way in which you made the journey to this place."

Then, perceiving the two piles of bank-notes, he exclaimed:

"Ah! I see! The million is here. We will not lose any time. Permit me."

"One moment," said the lawyer, placing himself before the table. "Mlle. Gerbois has not yet arrived."

"Well?"

"Is not her presence indispensable?"

"I understand! I understand! Arsène Lupin inspires only a limited confidence. He might pocket the half-million and not restore the hostage. Ah! Monsieur, people do not understand me. Because I have been obliged, by force of circumstances, to commit certain actions a little... out of the ordinary, my good faith is impugned... I, who have always observed the utmost scrupulosity and delicacy in business affairs. Besides, my dear monsieur if you have any fear, open the window and call. There are at least a dozen detectives in the street."

"Do you think so?"

Arsène Lupin raised the curtain.

"I think that Monsieur Gerbois could not throw Ganimard off the scent... What did I tell you? There he is now."

"Is it possible!" exclaimed the professor. "But I swear to you—"

"That you have not betrayed me?... I do not doubt you, but those fellows are clever—sometimes. Ah! I can see Folenfant, and Greaume, and Dieuzy—all good friends of mine!"

Mon. Detinan looked at Lupin in amazement. What assurance! He laughed as merrily as if engaged in some childish sport, as if no danger threatened him. This unconcern reassured the lawyer more than the presence of the detectives. He left the table on which the bank-notes were lying. Arsène Lupin picked up one pile of bills after the other, took from each of them twenty-five bank-notes which he offered to Mon. Detinan, saying:

"The reward of your services to Monsieur Gerbois and Arsène Lupin. You well deserve it."

"You owe me nothing," replied the lawyer.

"What! After all the trouble we have caused you!"

"And all the pleasure you have given me!"

"That means, my dear monsieur, that you do not wish to accept anything from Arsène Lupin. See what it is to have a bad reputation."

He then offered the fifty thousand francs to Mon. Gerbois, saying:

"Monsieur, in memory of our pleasant interview, permit me to return you this as a wedding-gift to Mlle. Gerbois."

Mon. Gerbois took the money, but said:

"My daughter will not marry."

"She will not marry if you refuse your consent; but she wishes to marry."

"What do you know about it?"

"I know that young girls often dream of such things unknown to their parents. Fortunately, there are sometimes good genii like Arsène Lupin who discover their little secrets in the drawers of their writing desks."

"Did you find anything else?" asked the lawyer. "I confess I am curious to know why you took so much trouble to get possession of that desk."

"On account of its historic interest, my friend. Although despite the opinion of Monsieur Gerbois, the desk contained no treasure except the lottery ticket—and that was unknown to me—I had been seeking it for a long time. That writing-desk of yew and mahogany was discovered in the little house in which Marie Walêwska once lived in Boulogne, and, on one of the drawers there is this inscription: '*Dedicated to Napoleon I, Emperor of the French, by his very faithful servant, Mancion.*' And above it, these words, engraved with the point of a knife: 'To you, Marie.' Afterwards, Napoleon had a similar desk made for the Empress Josephine; so that the secretary that was so much admired at the Malmaison was only an imperfect copy of the one that will henceforth form part of my collection."

"Ah! If I had known, when in the shop, I would gladly have given it up to you," said the professor.

Arsène Lupin smiled, as he replied:

"And you would have had the advantage of keeping for your own use lottery ticket number 514."

"And you would not have found it necessary to abduct my daughter."

"Abduct your daughter?"

"Yes."

"My dear monsieur, you are mistaken. Mlle. Gerbois was not abducted."

"No?"

"Certainly not. Abduction means force or violence. And I assure you that she served as hostage of her own free will."

"Of her own free will!" repeated Mon. Gerbois, in amazement.

"In fact, she almost asked to be taken. Why, do you suppose that an intelligent young girl like Mlle. Gerbois, and who, moreover, nourishes an unacknowledged passion, would hesitate to do what was necessary to secure her dowry. Ah! I swear to you it was not difficult to make her understand that it was the only way to overcome your obstinacy."

Mon. Detinan was greatly amused. He replied to Lupin:

"But I should think it was more difficult to get her to listen to you. How did you approach her?"

"Oh! I didn't approach her myself. I have not the honour of her acquaintance. A friend of mine, a lady, carried on the negotiations."

"The blonde woman in the automobile, no doubt."

"Precisely. All arrangements were made at the first interview near the college. Since then, Mlle. Gerbois and her new friend have been travelling in Belgium and Holland in a manner that should prove most pleasing and instructive to a young girl. She will tell you all about it herself—"

The bell of the vestibule door rang, three rings in quick succession, followed by two isolated rings.

"It is she," said Lupin. "Monsieur Detinan, if you will be so kind—"

The lawyer hastened to the door.

Two young women entered. One of them threw herself into the arms of Mon. Gerbois. The other approached Lupin. The latter was a tall woman of a good figure, very pale complexion, and with blond hair, parted over her forehead in undulating waves, that glistened and shone like the setting sun. She was dressed in black, with no display of jewelled ornaments; but, on the contrary, her appearance indicated good taste and refined elegance. Arsène Lupin spoke a few words to her; then, bowing to Mlle. Gerbois, he said:

"I owe you an apology, mademoiselle, for all your troubles, but I hope you have not been too unhappy—"

"Unhappy! Why, I should have been very happy, indeed, if it hadn't been for leaving my poor father."

"Then all is for the best. Kiss him again, and take advantage of the opportunity—it is an excellent one—to speak to him about your cousin."

"My cousin! What do you mean? I don't understand."

"Of course, you understand. Your cousin Philippe. The young man whose letters you kept so carefully."

Suzanne blushed; but, following Lupin's advice, she again threw herself into her father's arms. Lupin gazed upon them with a tender look.

"Ah! Such is my reward for a virtuous act! What a touching picture! A happy father and a happy daughter! And to know that their joy is your work, Lupin! Hereafter these people will bless you, and reverently transmit your name unto their descendants, even unto the fourth generation. What a glorious reward, Lupin, for one act of kindness!"

He walked to the window.

"Is dear old Ganimard still waiting?... He would like very much to be present at this charming domestic scene!... Ah! he is not there... Nor any of the others... I don't see anyone. The deuce! The situation is becoming serious. I dare say they are already under the porte-cochere... talking to the concierge, perhaps... or, even, ascending the stairs!"

Mon. Gerbois made a sudden movement. Now, that his daughter had been restored to him, he saw the situation in a different light. To him, the arrest of his adversary meant half-a-million francs. Instinctively, he made a step forward. As if by chance, Lupin stood in his way.

"Where are you going, Monsieur Gerbois? To defend me against them! That is very kind of you, but I assure you it is not necessary. They are more worried than I."

Then he continued to speak, with calm deliberation:

"But, really, what do they know? That you are here, and, perhaps, that Mlle. Gerbois is here, for they may have seen her arrive with an unknown lady. But they do not imagine that I am here. How is it possible that I could be in a house that they ransacked from cellar to garret this morning? They suppose that the unknown lady was sent by me to make the exchange, and they will be ready to arrest her when she goes out—"

At that moment, the bell rang. With a brusque movement, Lupin seized Mon. Gerbois, and said to him, in an imperious tone:

"Do not move! Remember your daughter, and be prudent— otherwise—As to you, Monsieur Detinan, I have your promise."

Mon. Gerbois was rooted to the spot. The lawyer did not stir. Without the least sign of haste, Lupin picked up his hat and brushed the dust from off it with his sleeve.

"My dear Monsieur Detinan, if I can ever be of service to you... My best wishes, Mademoiselle Suzanne, and my kind regards to Monsieur Philippe."

He drew a heavy gold watch from his pocket.

"Monsieur Gerbois, it is now forty-two minutes past three. At forty-six minutes past three, I give you permission to leave this room. Not one minute sooner than forty-six minutes past three."

"But they will force an entrance," suggested Mon. Detinan.

"You forget the law, my dear monsieur! Ganimard would never venture to violate the privacy of a French citizen. But, pardon me, time flies, and you are all slightly nervous."

He placed his watch on the table, opened the door of the room and addressing the blonde lady he said:

"Are you ready my dear?"

He drew back to let her pass, bowed respectfully to Mlle. Gerbois, and went out, closing the door behind him. Then they heard him in the vestibule, speaking, in a loud voice: "Good-day, Ganimard, how goes it? Remember me to Madame Ganimard. One of these days, I shall invite her to breakfast. Au revoir, Ganimard."

The bell rang violently, followed by repeated rings, and voices on the landing.

"Forty-five minutes," muttered Mon. Gerbois.

After a few seconds, he left the room and stepped into the vestibule. Arsène Lupin and the blonde lady had gone.

"Papa!... you mustn't! Wait!" cried Suzanne.

"Wait! you are foolish!... No quarter for that rascal!... And the half-million?"

He opened the outer door. Ganimard rushed in.

"That woman—where is she? And Lupin?"

"He was here... he is here."

Ganimard uttered a cry of triumph.

"We have him. The house is surrounded."

"But the servant's stairway?" suggested Mon. Detinan.

"It leads to the court," said Ganimard. "There is only one exit—the street-door. Ten men are guarding it."

"But he didn't come in by the street-door, and he will not go out that way."

"What way, then?" asked Ganimard. "Through the air?"

He drew aside a curtain and exposed a long corridor leading to the kitchen. Ganimard ran along it and tried the door of the servants' stairway. It was locked. From the window he called to one of his assistants:

"Seen anyone?"

"No."

"Then they are still in the house!" he exclaimed. "They are hiding in one of the rooms! They cannot have escaped. Ah! Lupin, you fooled me before, but, this time, I get my revenge."

At seven o'clock in the evening, Mon. Dudonis, chief of the detective service, astonished at not receiving any news, visited the rue Clapeyron. He questioned the detectives who were guarding the house, then ascended to Mon. Detinan's apartment. The lawyer led him into his room. There, Mon. Dudonis beheld a man, or rather two legs kicking in the air, while the body to which they belonged was hidden in the depths of the chimney.

"Ohé!... Ohé!" gasped a stifled voice. And a more distant voice, from on high, replied:

"Ohé!... Ohé!"

Mon. Dudonis laughed, and exclaimed:

"Here! Ganimard, have you turned chimney-sweep?"

The detective crawled out of the chimney. With his blackened face, his sooty clothes, and his feverish eyes, he was quite unrecognizable.

"I am looking for *him*," he growled.

"Who?"

"Arsène Lupin... and his friend."

"Well, do you suppose they are hiding in the chimney?"

Ganimard arose, laid his sooty hand on the sleeve of his superior officer's coat, and exclaimed, angrily:

"Where do you think they are, chief? They must be somewhere! They are flesh and blood like you and me, and can't fade away like smoke."

"No, but they have faded away just the same."

"But how? How? The house is surrounded by our men—even on the roof."

"What about the adjoining house?"

"There's no communication with it."

"And the apartments on the other floors?"

"I know all the tenants. They have not seen anyone."

"Are you sure you know all of them?"

"Yes. The concierge answers for them. Besides, as an extra precaution, I have placed a man in each apartment. They can't escape. If I don't get them to-night, I will get them tomorrow. I shall sleep here."

He slept there that night and the two following nights. Three days and nights passed away without the discovery of the irrepressible Lupin or his female companion; more than that, Ganimard did not unearth the slightest clue on which to base a theory to explain their escape. For that reason, he adhered to his first opinion.

"There is no trace of their escape; therefore, they are here."

It may be that, at the bottom of his heart, his conviction was less firmly established, but he would not confess it. No, a thousand times, no! A man and a woman could not vanish like the evil spirits in a fairy tale. And, without losing his courage, he continued his searches, as if he expected to find the fugitives concealed in some impenetrable retreat, or embodied in the stone walls of the house.

Chapter 2

THE BLUE DIAMOND

ON the evening of March 27, at number 134 avenue Henri-Martin, in the house that he had inherited from his brother six months before, the old general Baron d'Hautrec, ambassador at Berlin under the second Empire, was asleep in a comfortable armchair, while his secretary was reading to him, and the Sister Auguste was warming his bed and preparing the night-lamp. At eleven o'clock, the Sister, who was obliged to return to the convent of her order at that hour, said to the secretary:

"Mademoiselle Antoinette, my work is finished; I am going."

"Very well, Sister."

"Do not forget that the cook is away, and that you are alone in the house with the servant."

"Have no fear for the Baron. I sleep in the adjoining room and always leave the door open."

The Sister left the house. A few moments later, Charles, the servant, came to receive his orders. The Baron was now awake, and spoke for himself.

"The usual orders, Charles: see that the electric bell rings in your room, and, at the first alarm, run for the doctor. Now, Mademoiselle Antoinette, how far did we get in our reading?"

"Is Monsieur not going to bed now?"

"No, no, I will go later. Besides, I don't need anyone."

Twenty minutes later, he was sleeping again, and Antoinette crept away on tiptoe. At that moment, Charles was closing the shutters on the lower floor. In the kitchen, he bolted the door leading to the garden, and, in the vestibule, he not only locked the door but hooked the chain as well. Then he ascended to his room on the third floor, went to bed, and was soon asleep.

Probably an hour had passed, when he leaped from his bed in alarm. The bell was ringing. It rang for some time, seven or eight seconds perhaps, without intermission.

"Well?" muttered Charles, recovering his wits, "another of the Baron's whims."

He dressed himself quickly, descended the stairs, stopped in front of the door, and rapped, according to his custom. He received no reply. He opened the door and entered.

"Ah! No light," he murmured. "What is that for?"

Then, in a low voice, he called:

"Mademoiselle?"

No reply.

"Are you there, mademoiselle? What's the matter? Is Monsieur le Baron ill?"

No reply. Nothing but a profound silence that soon became depressing. He took two steps forward; his foot struck a chair, and, having touched it, he noticed that it was overturned. Then, with his hand, he discovered other objects on the floor—a small table and a screen. Anxiously, he approached the wall, felt for the electric button, and turned on the light.

In the centre of the room, between the table and dressing-case, lay the body of his master, the Baron d'Hautrec.

"What!... It can't be possible!" he stammered.

He could not move. He stood there, with bulging eyes, gazing stupidly at the terrible disorder, the overturned chairs, a large crystal candelabra shattered in a thousand pieces, the clock lying on the marble hearthstone, all evidence of a fearful and desperate struggle. The handle of a stiletto glittered, not far from the corpse; the blade was stained with blood. A handkerchief, marked with red spots, was lying on the edge of the bed.

Charles recoiled with horror: the body lying at his feet extended itself for a moment, then shrunk up again; two or three tremors, and that was the end.

He stooped over the body. There was a clean-cut wound on the neck from which the blood was flowing and then congealing in a black pool on the carpet. The face retained an expression of extreme terror.

"Someone has killed him!" he muttered, "someone has killed him!"

Then he shuddered at the thought that there might be another dreadful crime. Did not the baron's secretary sleep in the adjoining room! Had not the assassin killed her also! He opened the door; the room was empty. He concluded that Antoinette had been abducted, or else she had gone away before the crime. He returned to the baron's chamber, his glance falling on the secretary, he noticed that that article of furniture remained intact. Then, he saw upon a table, beside a bunch of keys and a pocketbook that the baron placed there every night, a handful of golden louis. Charles seized the pocketbook, opened it, and found some bank-notes. He counted them; there were thirteen notes of one hundred francs each.

Instinctively, mechanically, he put the bank-notes in his pocket, rushed down the stairs, drew the bolt, unhooked the chain, closed the door behind him, and fled to the street.

Charles was an honest man. He had scarcely left the gate, when, cooled by the night air and the rain, he came to a sudden halt. Now, he saw his action in its true light, and it filled him with horror. He hailed a passing cab, and said to the driver:

"Go to the police-office, and bring the commissary. Hurry! There has been a murder in that house."

The cab-driver whipped his horse. Charles wished to return to the house, but found the gate locked. He had closed it himself when he came out, and it could not be opened from the outside. On the other hand, it was useless to ring, as there was no one in the house.

It was almost an hour before the arrival of the police. When they came, Charles told his story and handed the bank-notes to the commissary. A locksmith was summoned, and, after considerable difficulty, he succeeded in forcing open the garden gate and the vestibule door. The commissary of police entered the room first, but, immediately, turned to Charles and said:

"You told me that the room was in the greatest disorder."

Charles stood at the door, amazed, bewildered; all the furniture had been restored to its accustomed place. The small table was standing between the two windows, the chairs were upright, and the clock was on the centre of the mantel. The debris of the candelabra had been removed.

"Where is... Monsieur le Baron?" stammered Charles.

"That's so!" exclaimed the officer, "where is the victim?"

He approached the bed, and drew aside a large sheet, under which reposed the Baron d'Hautrec, formerly French Ambassador at Berlin. Over him, lay his military coat, adorned with the Cross of Honor. His features were calm. His eyes were closed.

"Someone has been here," said Charles.

"How did they get in?"

"I don't know, but someone has been here during my absence. There was a stiletto on the floor—there! And a handkerchief, stained with blood, on the bed. They are not here now. They have been carried away. And some one has put the room in order."

"Who would do that?"

"The assassin."

"But we found all the doors locked."

"He must have remained in the house."

"Then he must be here yet, as you were in front of the house all the time."

Charles reflected a moment, then said, slowly:

"Yes ... of course... I didn't go away from the gate."

"Who was the last person you saw with the baron?"

"Mademoiselle Antoinette, his secretary."

"What has become of her?"

"I don't know. Her bed wasn't occupied, so she must have gone out. I am not surprised at that, as she is young and pretty."

"But how could she leave the house?"

"By the door," said Charles.

"But you had bolted and chained it."

"Yes, but she must have left before that."

"And the crime was committed after her departure?"

"Of course," said the servant.

The house was searched from cellar to garret, but the assassin had fled. How? And when? Was it he or an accomplice who had returned to the scene of the crime and removed everything that might furnish a clue to his identity? Such were the questions the police were called upon to solve.

The coroner came at seven o'clock; and, at eight o'clock, Mon. Dudouis, the head of the detective service, arrived on the scene. They were followed by the Procureur of the Republic and the investigating magistrate. In addition to these officials, the house was overrun with policemen, detectives, newspaper reporters, photographers, and relatives and acquaintances of the murdered man.

A thorough search was made; they studied out the position of the corpse according to the information furnished by Charles; they questioned Sister Auguste when she arrived; but they discovered nothing new. Sister Auguste was astonished to learn of the disappearance of Antoinette Bréhat. She had engaged the young girl twelve days before, on excellent recommendations, and refused to believe that she would neglect her duty by leaving the house during the night.

"But, you see, she hasn't returned yet," said the magistrate, "and we are still confronted with the question: yyWhat has become of her?"

"I think she was abducted by the assassin," said Charles.

The theory was plausible, and was borne out by certain facts. Mon. Dudouis agreed with it. He said:

"Abducted? Ma foi! that is not improbable."

"Not only improbable," said a voice, "but absolutely opposed to the facts. There is not a particle of evidence to support such a theory."

The voice was harsh, the accent sharp, and no one was surprised to learn that the speaker was Ganimard. In no one else, would they tolerate such a domineering tone.

"Ah! it is you, Ganimard!" exclaimed Mon. Dudouis. "I had not seen you before."

"I have been here since two o'clock."

"So you are interested in some things outside of lottery ticket number 514, the affair of the rue Clapeyron, the blonde lady and Arsène Lupin?"

"Ha-ha!" laughed the veteran detective. "I would not say that Lupin is a stranger to the present case. But let us forget the affair of the lottery ticket for a few moments, and try to unravel this new mystery."

Ganimard is not one of those celebrated detectives whose methods will create a school, or whose name will be immortalized in the criminal annals of his country. He is devoid of those flashes of genius which characterize the work of Dupin, Lecoq and Sherlock Holmes. Yet, it must be admitted, he possesses superior qualities of observation, sagacity, perseverance and even intuition. His merit lies in his absolute independence. Nothing troubles or influences him, except, perhaps, a sort of fascination that Arsène Lupin holds over him. However that may be, there is no doubt that his position on that morning, in the house of the late Baron d'Hautrec, was one of undoubted superiority, and his collaboration in the case was appreciated and desired by the investigating magistrate.

"In the first place," said Ganimard, "I will ask Monsieur Charles to be very particular on one point: He says that, on the occasion of his first visit to the room, various articles of furniture were overturned and strewn about the place; now, I ask him whether, on his second visit to the room, he found all those articles restored to their accustomed places—I mean, of course, correctly placed."

"Yes, all in their proper places," replied Charles.

"It is obvious, then, that the person who replaced them must have been familiar with the location of those articles."

The logic of this remark was apparent to his hearers. Ganimard continued:

"One more question, Monsieur Charles. You were awakened by the ringing of your bell. Now, who, do you think, rang it?"

"Monsieur le baron, of course."

"When could he ring it?"

"After the struggle... when he was dying."

"Impossible; because you found him lying, unconscious, at a point more than four metres from the bell-button."

"Then he must have rung during the struggle."

"Impossible," declared Ganimard, "since the ringing, as you have said, was continuous and uninterrupted, and lasted seven or eight seconds. Do you think his antagonist would have permitted him to ring the bell in that leisurely manner?"

"Well, then, it was before the attack."

"Also, quite impossible, since you have told us that the lapse of time between the ringing of the bell and your entrance to the room was not more than three minutes. Therefore, if the baron rang before the attack, we are forced to the conclusion that the struggle, the murder and the flight of the assassin, all occurred within the short space of three minutes. I repeat: that is impossible."

"And yet," said the magistrate, "someone rang. If it were not the baron, who was it?"

"The murderer."

"For what purpose?"

"I do not know. But the fact that he did ring proves that he knew that the bell communicated with the servant's room. Now, who would know that, except an inmate of the house?"

Ganimard was drawing the meshes of his net closer and tighter. In a few clear and logical sentences, he had unfolded and defined his theory of the crime, so that it seemed quite natural when the magistrate said:

"As I understand it, Ganimard, you suspect the girl Antoinette Bréhat?"

"I do not suspect her; I accuse her."

"You accuse her of being an accomplice?"

"I accuse her of having killed Baron d'Hautrec."

"Nonsense! What proof have you?"

"The handful of hair I found in the right hand of the victim."

He produced the hair; it was of a beautiful blonde colour, and glittered like threads of gold. Charles looked at it, and said:

"That is Mademoiselle Antoinette's hair. There can be no doubt of it. And, then, there is another thing. I believe that the knife, which I saw on my first visit to the room, belonged to her. She used it to cut the leaves of books."

A long, dreadful silence followed, as if the crime had acquired an additional horror by reason of having been committed by a woman. At last, the magistrate said:

"Let us assume, until we are better informed, that the baron was killed by Antoinette Bréhat. We have yet to learn where she concealed herself after the crime, how she managed to return after Charles left the house, and how she made her escape after the arrival of the police. Have you formed any opinion on those points Ganimard?"

"None."

"Well, then, where do we stand?"

Ganimard was embarrassed. Finally, with a visible effort, he said:

"All I can say is that I find in this case the same method of procedure as we found in the affair of the lottery ticket number 514; the same phenomena, which might be termed the faculty of disappearing. Antoinette Bréhat has appeared and disappeared in this house as mysteriously as Arsène Lupin entered the house of Monsieur Detinan and escaped therefrom in the company of the blonde lady.

"Does that signify anything?"

"It does to me. I can see a probable connection between those two strange incidents. Antoinette Bréhat was hired by Sister Auguste twelve days ago, that is to say, on the day after the blonde Lady so cleverly slipped through my fingers. In the second place, the hair of the blonde Lady was exactly of the same brilliant golden hue as the hair found in this case."

"So that, in your opinion, Antoinette Bréhat—"

"Is the blonde Lady—precisely."

"And that Lupin had a hand in both cases?"

"Yes, that is my opinion."

This statement was greeted with an outburst of laughter. It came from Mon. Dudouis.

"Lupin! Always Lupin! Lupin is into everything; Lupin is everywhere!"

"Yes, Lupin is into everything of any consequence," replied Ganimard, vexed at the ridicule of his superior.

"Well, so far as I see," observed Mon. Dudouis, "you have not discovered any motive for this crime. The secretary was not broken into, nor the pocketbook carried away. Even, a pile of gold was left upon the table."

"Yes, that is so," exclaimed Ganimard, "but the famous diamond?"

"What diamond?"

"The blue diamond! The celebrated diamond which formed part of the royal crown of France, and which was given by the

Duke d'Aumale to Leonide Lebrun, and, at the death of Leonide Lebrun, was purchased by the Baron d'Hautrec as a souvenir of the charming comedienne that he had loved so well. That is one of those things that an old Parisian, like I, does not forget."

"It is obvious that if the blue diamond is not found, the motive for the crime is disclosed," said the magistrate. "But where should we search for it?"

"On the baron's finger," replied Charles. "He always wore the blue diamond on his left hand."

"I saw that hand, and there was only a plain gold ring on it," said Ganimard, as he approached the corpse.

"Look in the palm of the hand," replied the servant.

Ganimard opened the stiffened hand. The bezel was turned inward, and, in the centre of that bezel, the blue diamond shone with all its glorious splendour.

"The deuce!" muttered Ganimard, absolutely amazed, "I don't understand it."

"You will now apologize to Lupin for having suspected him, eh?" said Mon. Dudouis, laughing.

Ganimard paused for a moment's reflection, and then replied, sententiously:

"It is only when I do not understand things that I suspect Arsène Lupin."

Such were the facts established by the police on the day after the commission of that mysterious crime. Facts that were vague and incoherent in themselves, and which were not explained by any subsequent discoveries. The movements of Antoinette Bréhat remained as inexplicable as those of the blonde Lady, and the police discovered no trace of that mysterious creature with the golden hair who had killed Baron d'Hautrec and had failed to take from his finger the famous diamond that had once shone in the royal crown of France.

The heirs of the Baron d'Hautrec could not fail to benefit by such notoriety. They established in the house an exhibition of the furniture and other objects which were to be sold at the auction rooms of Drouot & Co. Modern furniture of indifferent taste, various objects of no artistic value... but, in the centre of the room, in a case of purple velvet, protected by a glass globe, and guarded by two officers, was the famous blue diamond ring.

A large magnificent diamond of incomparable purity, and of that indefinite blue which the clear water receives from an unclouded sky, of that blue which can be detected in the whiteness of linen. Some admired, some enthused... and some looked with horror on the chamber of the victim, on the spot where the corpse had lain, on the floor divested of its blood-stained carpet, and especially the walls, the unsurmountable walls over which the criminal must have passed. Some assured themselves that the marble mantel did not move, others imagined gaping holes, mouths of tunnels, secret connections with the sewers, and the catacombs—

The sale of the blue diamond took place at the salesroom of Drouot & Co. The place was crowded to suffocation, and the bidding was carried to the verge of folly. The sale was attended by all those who usually appear at similar events in Paris; those who buy, and those who make a pretence of being able to buy; bankers, brokers, artists, women of all classes, two cabinet ministers, an Italian tenor, an exiled king who, in order to maintain his credit, bid, with much ostentation, and in a loud voice, as high as one hundred thousand francs. One hundred thousand francs! He could offer that sum without any danger of his bid being accepted. The

Italian tenor risked one hundred and fifty thousand, and a member of the Comédie-Française bid one hundred and seventy-five thousand francs.

When the bidding reached two hundred thousand francs, the smaller competitors fell out of the race. At two hundred and fifty thousand, only two bidders remained in the field: Herschmann, the well-known capitalist, the king of gold mines; and the Countess de Crozon, the wealthy American, whose collection of diamonds and precious stones is famed throughout the world.

"Two hundred and sixty thousand ... two hundred and seventy thousand ... seventy-five ... eighty..." exclaimed the auctioneer, as he glanced at the two competitors in succession. "Two hundred and eighty thousand for madame... Do I hear any more?"

"Three hundred thousand," said Herschmann.

There was a short silence. The countess was standing, smiling, but pale from excitement. She was leaning against the back of the chair in front of her. She knew, and so did everyone present, that the issue of the duel was certain; logically, inevitably, it must terminate to the advantage of the capitalist, who had untold millions with which to indulge his caprices. However, the countess made another bid:

"Three hundred and five thousand."

Another silence. All eyes were now directed to the capitalist in the expectation that he would raise the bidding. But Herschmann was not paying any attention to the sale; his eyes were fixed on a sheet of paper which he held in his right hand, while the other hand held a torn envelope.

"Three hundred and five thousand," repeated the auctioneer. "Once!... Twice!... For the last time... Do I hear any more?... Once!... Twice!... Am I offered any more? Last chance!..."

Herschmann did not move.

"Third and last time!... Sold!" exclaimed the auctioneer, as his hammer fell.

"Four hundred thousand," cried Herschman, starting up, as if the sound of the hammer had roused him from his stupor.

Too late; the auctioneer's decision was irrevocable. Some of Herschmann's acquaintances pressed around him. What was the matter? Why did he not speak sooner? He laughed. and said:

"Ma foi! I simply forgot—in a moment of abstraction."

"That is strange."

"You see, I just received a letter."

"And that letter was sufficient—"

"To distract my attention? Yes, for a moment."

Ganimard was there. He had come to witness the sale of the ring. He stopped one of the attendants of the auction room, and said:

"Was it you who carried the letter to Monsieur Herschmann?"

"Yes."

"Who gave it to you?"

"A lady."

"Where is she?"

"Where is she?... She was sitting down there... the lady who wore a thick veil."

"She has gone?"

"Yes, just this moment."

Ganimard hastened to the door, and saw the lady descending the stairs. He ran after her. A crush of people delayed him at the entrance. When he reached the sidewalk, she had disappeared. He returned to the auction room, accosted Herschmann, introduced himself, and enquired about the letter. Herschmann handed it to him. It was carelessly scribbled in pencil, in a handwriting unknown to the capitalist, and contained these few words:

"The blue diamond brings misfortune. Remember the Baron d'Hautrec."

The vicissitudes of the blue diamond were not yet at an end. Although it had become well-known through the murder of the Baron d'Hautrec and the incidents at the auction-rooms, it was six months later that it attained even greater celebrity. During the following summer, the Countess de Crozon was robbed of the famous jewel she had taken so much trouble to acquire.

Let me recall that strange affair, of which the exciting and dramatic incidents sent a thrill through all of us, and over which I am now permitted to throw some light.

On the evening of August 10, the guests of the Count and Countess de Crozon were assembled in the drawing-room of the magnificent château which overlooks the Bay de Somme. To entertain her friends, the countess seated herself at the piano to play for them, after first placing her jewels on a small table near the piano, and, amongst them, was the ring of the Baron d'Hautrec.

An hour later, the count and the majority of the guests retired, including his two cousins and Madame de Réal, an intimate friend of the countess. The latter remained in the drawing-room with Herr Bleichen, the Austrian consul, and his wife.

They conversed for a time, and then the countess extinguished the large lamp that stood on a table in the centre of the room. At the same moment, Herr Bleichen extinguished the two piano lamps. There was a momentary darkness; then the consul lighted a candle, and the three of them retired to their rooms. But, as soon as she reached her apartment, the countess remembered her jewels and sent her maid to get them. When the maid returned with the jewels, she placed them on the mantel without the countess looking at them. Next day, Madame de Crozon found that one of her rings was missing; it was the blue diamond ring.

She informed her husband, and, after talking it over, they reached the conclusion that the maid was above suspicion, and that the guilty party must be Herr Bleichen.

The count notified the commissary of police at Amiens, who commenced an investigation and, discreetly, exercised a strict surveillance over the Austrian consul to prevent his disposing of the ring.

The château was surrounded by detectives day and night. Two weeks passed without incident. Then Herr Bleichen announced his intended departure. That day, a formal complaint was entered against him. The police made an official examination of his luggage. In a small satchel, the key to which was always carried by the consul himself, they found a bottle of dentifrice, and in that bottle they found the ring.

Madame Bleichen fainted. Her husband was placed under arrest.

Everyone will remember the line of defence adopted by the accused man. He declared that the ring must have been placed there by the Count de Crozen as an act of revenge. He said:

"The count is brutal and makes his wife very unhappy. She consulted me, and I advised her to get a divorce. The count heard of it in some way, and, to be revenged on me, he took the ring and placed it in my satchel."

The count and countess persisted in pressing the charge. Between the explanation which they gave and that of the consul, both equally possible and equally probable, the public had to choose. No new fact was discovered to turn the scale in either direction. A month of gossip, conjectures and investigations failed to produce a single ray of light.

Wearied of the excitement and notoriety, and incapable of securing the evidence necessary to sustain their charge against the consul, the count and countess at last sent to Paris for a detective competent to unravel the tangled threads of this mysterious skein. This brought Ganimard into the case.

For four days, the veteran detective searched the house from top to bottom, examined every foot of the ground, had long conferences with the maid, the chauffeur, the gardeners, the employees in the neighbouring post-offices, visited the rooms that had been occupied by the various guests. Then, one morning, he disappeared without taking leave of his host or hostess. But a week later, they received this telegram:

"Please come to the Japanese Tea-room, rue Boissy d'Anglas, tomorrow, Friday, evening at five o'clock. Ganimard."

At five o'clock, Friday evening, their automobile stopped in front of number nine rue Boissy-d'Anglas. The old detective was standing on the sidewalk, waiting for them. Without a word, he conducted them to the first floor of the Japanese Tea-room. In one of the rooms, they met two men, whom Ganimard introduced in these words:

"Monsieur Gerbois, professor in the College of Versailles, from whom, you will remember, Arsène Lupin stole half a million; Monsieur Léonce d'Hautrec, nephew and sole legatee of the Baron d'Hautrec."

A few minutes later, another man arrived. It was Mon. Dudouis, head of the detective service, and he appeared to be in a particularly bad temper. He bowed, and then said:

"What's the trouble now, Ganimard? I received your telephone message asking me to come here. Is it anything of consequence?"

"Yes, chief, it is a very important matter. Within an hour, the last two cases to which I was assigned will have their dénouement here. It seemed to me that your presence was indispensable."

"And also the presence of Dieuzy and Folenfant, whom I noticed standing near the door as I came in?"

"Yes, chief."

"For what? Are you going to make an arrest, and you wish to do it with a flourish? Come, Ganimard, I am anxious to hear about it."

Ganimard hesitated a moment, then spoke with the obvious intention of making an impression on his hearers:

"In the first place, I wish to state that Herr Bleichen had nothing to do with the theft of the ring."

"Oh! Oh!" exclaimed Mon. Dudouis, "that is a bold statement and a very serious one."

"And is that all you have discovered?" asked the Count de Crozon.

"Not at all. On the second day after the theft, three of your guests went on an automobile trip as far as Crécy. Two of them visited the famous battlefield; and, while they were there, the third party paid a hasty visit to the post-office, and mailed a small box, tied and sealed according to the regulations, and declared its value to be one hundred francs."

"I see nothing strange in that," said the count.

"Perhaps you will see something strange in it when I tell you that this person, in place of giving her true name, sent the box under the name of Rousseau, and the person to whom it was addressed, a certain Monsieur Beloux of Paris, moved his place of residence immediately after receiving the box, in other words, the ring."

"I presume you refer to one of my cousins d'Andelle?"

"No," replied Ganimard.

"Madame de Réal, then?"

"Yes."

"You accuse my friend, Madam de Réal?" cried the countess, shocked and amazed.

"I wish to ask you one question, madame," said Ganimard. "Was Madam de Réal present when you purchased the ring?"

"Yes, but we did not go there together."

"Did she advise you to buy the ring?"

The countess considered for a moment, then said:

"Yes, I think she mentioned it first—"

"Thank you, madame. Your answer establishes the fact that it was Madame de Réal who was the first to mention the ring, and it was she who advised you to buy it."

"But, I consider my friend is quite incapable—"

"Pardon me, countess, when I remind you that Madame de Réal is only a casual acquaintance and not your intimate friend, as the newspapers have announced. It was only last winter that you met her for the first time. Now, I can prove that everything she has told you about herself, her past life, and her relatives, is absolutely false; that Madame Blanche de Réal had no actual existence before she met you, and she has now ceased to exist."

"Well?"

"Well?" replied Ganimard.

"Your story is a very strange one," said the countess, "but it has no application to our case. If Madame de Réal had taken the ring, how do you explain the fact that it was found in Herr Bleichen's tooth-powder? Anyone who would take the risk and trouble of stealing the blue diamond would certainly keep it. What do you say to that?"

"I—nothing—but Madame de Réal will answer it."

"Oh! She does exist, then?"

"She does—and does not. I will explain in a few words. Three days ago, while reading a newspaper, I glanced over the list of hotel arrivals at Trouville, and there I read: 'Hôtel Beaurivage— Madame de Réal, etc.'

"I went to Trouville immediately, and interviewed the proprietor of the hotel. From the description and other information I received from him, I concluded that she was the very Madame de Réal that I was seeking; but she had left the hotel, giving her address in Paris as number three rue de Colisée. The day before yesterday I went to that address, and learned that there was no person there called Madame de Réal, but there was a Madame Réal, living on the second floor, who acted as a diamond broker and was frequently away from home. She had returned from a journey on the preceding evening. Yesterday, I called on her and, under an assumed name, I offered to act as an intermedium in the sale of some diamonds to certain wealthy friends of mine. She is to meet me here to-day to carry out that arrangement."

"What! You expect her to come here?"

"Yes, at half-past five."

"Are you sure it is she?"

"Madame de Réal of the Château de Crozon? Certainly. I have convincing evidence of that fact. But... listen!... I hear Folenfant's signal."

It was a whistle. Ganimard arose quickly.

"There is no time to lose. Monsieur and Madame de Crozon, will you be kind enough to go into the next room. You also, Monsieur d'Hautrec, and you, Monsieur Gerbois. The door will remain open, and when I give the signal, you will come out. Of course, Chief, you will remain here."

"We may be disturbed by other people," said Mon. Dudouis.

"No. This is a new establishment, and the proprietor is one of my friends. He will not let anyone disturb us—except the blonde Lady."

"The blonde Lady! What do you mean?"

"Yes, the blonde Lady herself, chief; the friend and accomplice of Arsène Lupin, the mysterious blonde Lady against whom I hold convincing evidence; but, in addition to that, I wish to confront her with all the people she has robbed."

He looked through the window.

"I see her. She is coming in the door now. She can't escape: Folenfant and Dieuzy are guarding the door... The blonde Lady is captured at last, Chief!"

A moment later a woman appeared at the door; she was tall and slender, with a very pale complexion and bright golden hair. Ganimard trembled with excitement; he could not move, nor utter a word. She was there, in front of him, at his mercy! What a victory over Arsène Lupin! And what a revenge! And, at the same time, the victory was such an easy one that he asked himself if the blonde Lady would not yet slip through his fingers by one of those miracles that usually terminated the exploits of Arsène Lupin. She remained standing near the door, surprised at the silence, and looked about her without any display of suspicion or fear.

"She will get away! She will disappear!" thought Ganimard.

Then he managed to get between her and the door. She turned to go out.

"No, no!" he said. "Why are you going away?"

"Really, monsieur, I do not understand what this means. Allow me—"

"There is no reason why you should go, madame, and very good reasons why you should remain."

"But—"

"It is useless, madame. You cannot go."

Trembling, she sat on a chair, and stammered:

"What is it you want?"

Ganimard had won the battle and captured the blonde Lady. He said to her:

"Allow me to present the friend I mentioned, who desires to purchase some diamonds. Have you procured the stones you promised to bring?"

"No—no—I don't know. I don't remember."

"Come! Jog your memory! A person of your acquaintance intended to send you a tinted stone...' Something like the blue diamond,' I said, laughing; and you replied: 'Exactly, I expect to have just what you want.' Do you remember?"

She made no reply. A small satchel fell from her hand. She picked it up quickly, and held it securely. Her hands trembled slightly.

"Come!" said Ganimard, "I see you have no confidence in us, Madame de Réal. I shall set you a good example by showing you what I have."

He took from his pocketbook a paper which he unfolded, and disclosed a lock of hair.

"These are a few hairs torn from the head of Antoinette Bréhat by the Baron d'Hautrec, which I found clasped in his dead hand. I have shown them to Mlle. Gerbois, who declares they are of the exact colour of the hair of the blonde Lady. Besides, they are exactly the colour of your hair—the identical colour."

Madame Réal looked at him in bewilderment, as if she did not understand his meaning. He continued:

"And here are two perfume bottles, without labels, it is true, and empty, but still sufficiently impregnated with their odour to enable Mlle. Gerbois to recognize in them the perfume used by that blonde Lady who was her traveling companion for two weeks. Now, one of these bottles was found in the room that Madame de Réal occupied at the Château de Crozon, and the other in the room that you occupied at the Hôtel Beaurivage."

"What do you say?... The blonde Lady... the Château de Crozon..."

The detective did not reply. He took from his pocket and placed on the table, side by side, four small sheets of paper. Then he said:

"I have, on these four pieces of paper, various specimens of handwriting; the first is the writing of Antoinette Bréhat; the second was written by the woman who sent the note to Baron Herschmann at the auction sale of the blue diamond; the third is that of Madame de Réal, written while she was stopping at the Château de Crozon; and the fourth is your handwriting, madame ... it is your name and address, which you gave to the porter of the Hôtel Beaurivage at Trouville. Now, compare the four handwritings. They are identical."

"What absurdity is this? really, monsieur, I do not understand. What does it mean?"

"It means, madame," exclaimed Ganimard, "that the blonde Lady, the friend and accomplice of Arsène Lupin, is none other than you, Madame Réal."

Ganimard went to the adjoining room and returned with Mon. Gerbois, whom he placed in front of Madame Réal, as he said:

"Monsieur Gerbois, is this the person who abducted your daughter, the woman you saw at the house of Monsieur Detinan?"

"No."

Ganimard was so surprised that he could not speak for a moment; finally, he said: "No?... You must be mistaken..."

"I am not mistaken. Madame is blonde, it is true, and in that respect resembles the blonde Lady; but, in all other respects, she is totally different."

"I can't believe it. You must be mistaken."

Ganimard called in his other witnesses.

"Monsieur d'Hautrec," he said, "do you recognize Antoinette Bréhat?"

"No, this is not the person I saw at my uncle's house."

"This woman is not Madame de Réal," declared the Count de Crozon.

That was the finishing touch. Ganimard was crushed. He was buried beneath the ruins of the structure he had erected with so much care and assurance. His pride was humbled, his spirit was broken, by the force of this unexpected blow.

Mon. Dudouis arose, and said:

"We owe you an apology, madame, for this unfortunate mistake. But, since your arrival here, I have noticed your nervous agitation. Something troubles you; may I ask what it is?"

"Mon Dieu, monsieur, I was afraid. My satchel contains diamonds to the value of a hundred thousand francs, and the conduct of your friend was rather suspicious."

"But you were frequently absent from Paris. How do you explain that?"

"I make frequent journeys to other cities in the course of my business. That is all."

Mon. Dudouis had nothing more to ask. He turned to his subordinate, and said:

"Your investigation has been very superficial, Ganimard, and your conduct toward this lady is really deplorable. You will come to my office tomorrow and explain it."

The interview was at an end, and Mon. Dudouis was about to leave the room when a most annoying incident occurred. Madame Réal turned to Ganimard, and said:

"I understand that you are Monsieur Ganimard. Am I right?"

"Yes."

"Then, this letter must be for you. I received it this morning. It was addressed to 'Mon. Justin Ganimard, care of Madame Réal.' I thought it was a joke, because I did not know you under that name, but it appears that your unknown correspondent knew of our rendezvous."

Ganimard was inclined to put the letter in his pocket unread, but he dared not do so in the presence of his superior, so he opened the envelope and read the letter aloud, in an almost inaudible tone:

"Once upon a time, there were a blonde Lady, a Lupin, and a Ganimard. Now, the wicked Ganimard had evil designs on the pretty blonde Lady, and the good Lupin was her friend and protector. When the good Lupin wished the blonde Lady to become the friend of the Countess de Crozon, he caused her to assume the name of Madame de Réal, which is a close resemblance to the name of a certain diamond broker, a woman with a pale complexion and golden hair. And the good Lupin said to himself: If ever the wicked Ganimard gets upon the track of the blonde Lady, how useful it will be to me if he should be diverted to the track of the honest diamond broker. A wise precaution that has borne good fruit. A little note sent to the newspaper read by the wicked Ganimard, a perfume bottle intentionally forgotten by the genuine blonde Lady at the Hôtel Beaurivage, the name and address of Madame Réal written on the hotel register by the genuine blonde Lady, and the trick is played. What do you think of it, Ganimard! I wished to tell you the true story of this affair, knowing that you would be the first to laugh over it. Really, it is quite amusing, and I have enjoyed it very much.

"Accept my best wishes, dear friend, and give my kind regards to the worthy Mon. Dudouis.

"ARSÈNE LUPIN."

"He knows everything," muttered Ganimard, but he did not see the humour of the situation as Lupin had predicted. "He knows some things I have never mentioned to anyone. How could he find out that I was going to invite you here, chief? How could he know that I had found the first perfume bottle? How could he find out those things?"

He stamped his feet and tore his hair—a prey to the most tragic despair. Mon. Dudouis felt sorry for him, and said:

"Come, Ganimard, never mind; try to do better next time."

And Mon. Dudouis left the room, accompanied by Madame Réal.

During the next ten minutes, Ganimard read and re-read the letter of Arsène Lupin. Monsieur and Madame de Crozon, Monsieur d'Hautrec and Monsieur Gerbois were holding an animated discussion in a corner of the room. At last, the count approached the detective, and said:

"My dear monsieur, after your investigation, we are no nearer the truth than we were before."

"Pardon me, but my investigation has established these facts: that the blonde Lady is the mysterious heroine of these exploits, and that Arsène Lupin directed them."

"Those facts do not solve the mystery; in fact, they render it more obscure. The blonde Lady commits a murder in order to steal the blue diamond, and yet she does not steal it. Afterward she steals it and gets rid of it by secretly giving it to another person. How do you explain her strange conduct?"

"I cannot explain it."

"Of course; but, perhaps, someone else can."

"Who?"

The Count hesitated, so the Countess replied, frankly:

"There is only one man besides yourself who is competent to enter the arena with Arsène Lupin and overcome him. Have you any objection to our engaging the services of Herlock Sholmes in this case?"

Ganimard was vexed at the question, but stammered a reply:

"No... but... I do not understand what—"

"Let me explain. All this mystery annoys me. I wish to have it cleared up. Monsieur Gerbois and Monsieur d'Hautrec have the same desire, and we have agreed to send for the celebrated English detective."

"You are right, madame," replied the detective, with a loyalty that did him credit, "you are right. Old Ganimard is not able to overcome Arsène Lupin. But will Herlock Sholmes succeed? I hope so, as I have the greatest admiration for him. But... it is improbable."

"Do you mean to say that he will not succeed?"

"That is my opinion. I can foresee the result of a duel between Herlock Sholmes and Arsène Lupin. The Englishman will be defeated."

"But, in any event, can we count on your assistance?"

"Quite so, madame. I shall be pleased to render Monsieur Sholmes all possible assistance."

"Do you know his address?"

"Yes; 219 Parker street."

That evening Monsieur and Madame de Crozon withdrew the charge they had made against Herr Bleichen, and a joint letter was addressed to Herlock Sholmes.

Chapter 3

HERLOCK SHOLMES OPENS HOSTILITIES

"WHAT does monsieur wish?"

"Anything," replied Arsène Lupin, like a man who never worries over the details of a meal; "anything you like, but no meat or alcohol."

The waiter walked away, disdainfully.

"What! Still a vegetarian?" I exclaimed.

"More so than ever," replied Lupin.

"Through taste, faith, or habit?"

"Hygiene."

"And do you never fall from grace?"

"Oh! yes... when I am dining out... and wish to avoid being considered eccentric."

We were dining near the Northern Railway station, in a little restaurant to which Arsène Lupin had invited me. Frequently he would send me a telegram asking me to meet him in some obscure restaurant, where we could enjoy a quiet dinner, well served, and which was always made interesting to me by his recital of some startling adventure theretofore unknown to me.

On that particular evening he appeared to be in a more lively mood than usual. He laughed and joked with careless animation, and with that delicate sarcasm that was habitual with him—a light and spontaneous sarcasm that was quite free from any tinge of malice. It was a pleasure to find him in that jovial mood, and I could not resist the desire to tell him so.

"Ah! yes," he exclaimed, "there are days in which I find life as bright and gay as a spring morning; then life seems to be an infinite treasure which I can never exhaust. And yet God knows I lead a careless existence!"

"Too much so, perhaps."

"Ah! but I tell you, the treasure is infinite. I can spend it with a lavish hand. I can cast my youth and strength to the four winds of Heaven, and it is replaced by a still younger and greater force. Besides, my life is so pleasant!... If I wished to do so, I might become—what shall I say?... An orator, a manufacturer, a politician... But, I assure you, I shall never have such a desire. Arsène Lupin, I am; Arsène Lupin, I shall remain. I have made a vain search in history to find a career comparable to mine; a life better filled or more intense... Napoleon? Yes, perhaps... But Napoleon, toward the close of his career, when all Europe was trying to crush him, asked himself on the eve of each battle if it would not be his last."

Was he serious? Or was he joking? He became more animated as he proceeded:

"That is everything, do you understand, the danger! The continuous feeling of danger! To breathe it as you breathe the air, to scent it in every breath of wind, to detect it in every unusual sound... And, in the midst of the tempest, to remain calm ... and not to stumble! Otherwise, you are lost. There is only one sensation equal to it: that of the chauffeur in an automobile race. But that race lasts only a few hours; my race continues until death!"

"What fantasy!" I exclaimed. "And you wish me to believe that you have no particular motive for your adoption of that exciting life?"

"Come," he said, with a smile, "you are a clever psychologist. Work it out for yourself."

He poured himself a glass of water, drank it, and said:

"Did you read *'Le Temps'* today?"

"No."

"Herlock Sholmes crossed the Channel this afternoon, and arrived in Paris about six o'clock."

"The deuce! What is he coming for?"

"A little journey he has undertaken at the request of the Count and Countess of Crozon, Monsieur Gerbois, and the nephew of Baron d'Hautrec. They met him at the Northern Railway station, took him to meet Ganimard, and, at this moment, the six of them are holding a consultation."

Despite a strong temptation to do so, I had never ventured to question Arsène Lupin concerning any action of his private life, unless he had first mentioned the subject to me. Up to that moment his name had not been mentioned, at least officially, in connection with the blue diamond. Consequently, I consumed my curiosity in patience. He continued:

"There is also in *'Le Temps'* an interview with my old friend Ganimard, according to whom a certain blonde lady, who should be my friend, must have murdered the Baron d'Hautrec and tried to rob Madame de Crozon of her famous ring. And—what do you think?—he accuses me of being the instigator of those crimes."

I could not suppress a slight shudder. Was this true? Must I believe that his career of theft, his mode of existence, the logical result of such a life, had drawn that man into more serious crimes, including murder? I looked at him. He was so calm, and his eyes had such a frank expression! I observed his hands: they had been formed from a model of exceeding delicacy, long and slender; inoffensive, truly; and the hands of an artist...

"Ganimard has pipe-dreams," I said.

"No, no!" protested Lupin. "Ganimard has some cleverness; and, at times, almost inspiration."

"Inspiration!"

"Yes. For instance, that interview is a master-stroke. In the first place, he announces the coming of his English rival in order to put me on my guard, and make his task more difficult. In the second place, he indicates the exact point to which he has conducted the affair in order that Sholmes will not get credit for the work already done by Ganimard. That is good warfare."

"Whatever it may be, you have two adversaries to deal with, and such adversaries!"

"Oh! one of them doesn't count."

"And the other?"

"Sholmes? Oh! I confess he is a worthy foe; and that explains my present good humour. In the first place, it is a question of self-esteem; I am pleased to know that they consider me a subject worthy the attention of the celebrated English detective. In the next place, just imagine the pleasure a man, such as I, must experience in the thought of a duel with Herlock Sholmes. But I shall be obliged to strain every muscle; he is a clever fellow, and will contest every inch of the ground."

"Then you consider him a strong opponent?"

"I do. As a detective, I believe, he has never had an equal. But I have one advantage over him; he is making the attack and I am simply defending myself. My role is the easier one. Besides, I am familiar with his method of warfare, and he does not know mine. I am prepared to show him a few new tricks that will give him something to think about."

He tapped the table with his fingers as he uttered the following sentences, with an air of keen delight:

"Arsène Lupin against Herlock Sholmes... France against England... Trafalgar will be revenged at last... Ah! the rascal ... he doesn't suspect that I am prepared ... and a Lupin warned—"

He stopped suddenly, seized with a fit of coughing, and hid his face in his napkin, as if something had stuck in his throat.

"A bit of bread?" I inquired. "Drink some water."

"No, it isn't that," he replied, in a stifled voice.

"Then, what is it?"

"The want of air."

"Do you wish a window opened?"

"No, I shall go out. Give me my hat and overcoat, quick! I must go."

"What's the matter?"

"The two gentlemen who came in just now... Look at the taller one ... now, when we go out, keep to my left, so he will not see me."

"The one who is sitting behind you?"

"Yes. I will explain it to you, outside."

"Who is it?"

"Herlock Sholmes."

He made a desperate effort to control himself, as if he were ashamed of his emotion, replaced his napkin, drank a glass of water, and, quite recovered, said to me, smiling:

"It is strange, hein, that I should be affected so easily, but that unexpected sight—"

"What have you to fear, since no one can recognize you, on account of your many transformations? Every time I see you it seems to me your face is changed; it's not at all familiar. I don't know why."

"But *he* would recognize me," said Lupin. "He has seen me only once; but, at that time, he made a mental photograph of me— not of my external appearance but of my very soul—not what I appear to be but just what I am. Do you understand? And then ... and then... I did not expect to meet him here... Such a strange encounter!... in this little restaurant..."

"Well, shall we go out?"

"No, not now," said Lupin.

"What are you going to do?"

"The better way is to act frankly... to have confidence in him—trust him..."

"You will not speak to him?"

"Why not! It will be to my advantage to do so, and find out what he knows, and, perhaps, what he thinks. At present I have the feeling that his gaze is on my neck and shoulders, and that he is trying to remember where he has seen them before."

He reflected a moment. I observed a malicious smile at the corner of his mouth; then, obedient, I think, to a whim of his impulsive nature, and not to the necessities of the situation, he arose, turned around, and, with a bow and a joyous air, he said:

"By what lucky chance? Ah! I am delighted to see you. Permit me to introduce a friend of mine."

For a moment the Englishman was disconcerted; then he made a movement as if he would seize Arsène Lupin. The latter shook his head, and said:

"That would not be fair; besides, the movement would be an awkward one and ... quite useless."

The Englishman looked about him, as if in search of assistance.

"No use," said Lupin. "Besides, are you quite sure you can place your hand on me? Come, now, show me that you are a real Englishman and, therefore, a good sport."

This advice seemed to commend itself to the detective, for he partially rose and said, very formally:

"Monsieur Wilson, my friend and assistant—Monsieur Arsène Lupin."

Wilson's amazement evoked a laugh. With bulging eyes and gaping mouth, he looked from one to the other, as if unable to comprehend the situation. Herlock Sholmes laughed and said:

"Wilson, you should conceal your astonishment at an incident which is one of the most natural in the world."

"Why do you not arrest him?" stammered Wilson.

"Have you not observed, Wilson, that the gentleman is between me and the door, and only a few steps from the door. By the time I could move my little finger he would be outside."

"Don't let that make any difference," said Lupin, who now walked around the table and seated himself so that the Englishman was between him and the door—thus placing himself at the mercy of the foreigner.

Wilson looked at Sholmes to find out if he had the right to admire this act of wanton courage. The Englishman's face was impenetrable; but, a moment later, he called:

"Waiter!"

When the waiter came he ordered soda, beer and whisky. The treaty of peace was signed—until further orders. In a few moments the four men were conversing in an apparently friendly manner.

Herlock Sholmes is a man such as you might meet every day in the business world. He is about fifty years of age, and looks as if he might have passed his life in an office, adding up columns of dull figures or writing out formal statements of business accounts. There was nothing to distinguish him from the average citizen of London, except the appearance of his eyes, his terribly keen and penetrating eyes.

But then he is Herlock Sholmes—which means that he is a wonderful combination of intuition, observation, clairvoyance and ingenuity. One could readily believe that nature had been pleased to take the two most extraordinary detectives that the imagination of man has hitherto conceived, the Dupin of Edgar Allen Poe and the Lecoq of Emile Gaboriau, and, out of that material, constructed a new detective, more extraordinary and supernatural than either of them. And when a person reads the history of his exploits, which have made him famous throughout the entire world, he asks himself whether Herlock Sholmes is not a mythical personage, a fictitious hero born in the brain of a great novelist—Conan Doyle, for instance.

When Arsène Lupin questioned him in regard to the length of his sojourn in France he turned the conversation into its proper channel by saying:

"That depends on you, monsieur."

"Oh!" exclaimed Lupin, laughing, "if it depends on me you can return to England tonight."

"That is a little too soon, but I expect to return in the course of eight or nine days—ten at the outside."

"Are you in such a hurry?"

"I have many cases to attend to; such as the robbery of the Anglo-Chinese Bank, the abduction of Lady Eccleston... But, don't you think, Monsieur Lupin, that I can finish my business in Paris within a week?"

"Certainly, if you confine your efforts to the case of the blue diamond. It is, moreover, the length of time that I require to make preparations for my safety in case the solution of that affair should give you certain dangerous advantages over me."

"And yet," said the Englishman, "I expect to close the business in eight or ten days."

"And arrest me on the eleventh, perhaps?"

"No, the tenth is my limit."

Lupin shook his head thoughtfully, as he said:

"That will be difficult—very difficult."

"Difficult, perhaps, but possible, therefore certain—"

"Absolutely certain," said Wilson, as if he had clearly worked out the long series of operations which would conduct his collaborator to the desired result.

"Of course," said Herlock Sholmes, "I do not hold all the trump cards, as these cases are already several months old, and I lack certain information and clues upon which I am accustomed to base my investigations."

"Such as spots of mud and cigarette ashes," said Wilson, with an air of importance.

"In addition to the remarkable conclusions formed by Monsieur Ganimard, I have obtained all the articles written on the subject, and have formed a few deductions of my own."

"Some ideas which were suggested to us by analysis or hypothesis," added Wilson, sententiously.

"I wish to enquire," said Arsène Lupin, in that deferential tone which he employed in speaking to Sholmes, "would I be indiscreet if I were to ask you what opinion you have formed about the case?"

Really, it was a most exciting situation to see those two men facing each other across the table, engaged in an earnest discussion as if they were obliged to solve some abstruse problem or come to an agreement upon some controverted fact. Wilson was in the seventh heaven of delight. Herlock Sholmes filled his pipe slowly, lighted it, and said:

"This affair is much simpler than it appeared to be at first sight."

"Much simpler," said Wilson, as a faithful echo.

"I say 'this affair,' for, in my opinion, there is only one," said Sholmes. "The death of the Baron d'Hautrec, the story of the ring, and, let us not forget, the mystery of lottery ticket number 514, are only different phases of what one might call the mystery of the blonde Lady. Now, according to my view, it is simply a question of discovering the bond that unites those three episodes in the same story—the fact which proves the unity of the three events. Ganimard, whose judgment is rather superficial, finds that unity in the faculty of disappearance; that is, in the power of coming and going unseen and unheard. That theory does not satisfy me."

"Well, what is your idea?" asked Lupin.

"In my opinion," said Sholmes, "the characteristic feature of the three episodes is your design and purpose of leading the affair into a certain channel previously chosen by you. It is, on your part, more than a plan; it is a necessity, an indispensable condition of success."

"Can you furnish any details of your theory?"

"Certainly. For example, from the beginning of your conflict with Monsieur Gerbois, is it not evident that the apartment of Monsieur Detinan is the place selected by you, the inevitable spot where all the parties must meet? In your opinion, it was the only safe place, and you arranged a rendezvous there, publicly, one might say, for the blonde Lady and Mademoiselle Gerbois."

"The professor's daughter," added Wilson. "Now, let us consider the case of the blue diamond. Did you try to appropriate it while the Baron d'Hautrec possessed it! No. But the baron takes his brother's house. Six months later we have the intervention of Antoinette Bréhat and the first attempt. The diamond escapes you, and the sale is widely advertised to take place at the Drouot auction-rooms. Will it be a free and open sale? Is the richest amateur sure to carry off the jewel! No. Just as the banker Herschmann is on the point of buying the ring, a lady sends him a letter of warning, and it is the Countess de Crozon, prepared and influenced by the same lady, who becomes the purchaser of the diamond. Will the ring disappear at once? No; you lack the opportunity. Therefore, you must wait. At last the Countess goes to her château. That is what you were waiting for. The ring disappears."

"To reappear again in the tooth-powder of Herr Bleichen," remarked Lupin.

"Oh! such nonsense!" exclaimed Sholmes, striking the table with his fist, "don't tell me such a fairy tale. I am too old a fox to be led away by a false scent."

"What do you mean?"

"What do I mean?" said Sholmes, then paused a moment as if he wished to arrange his effect. At last he said:

"The blue diamond that was found in the tooth-powder was false. You kept the genuine stone."

Arsène Lupin remained silent for a moment; then, with his eyes fixed on the Englishman, he replied, calmly:

"You are impertinent, monsieur."

"Impertinent, indeed!" repeated Wilson, beaming with admiration.

"Yes," said Lupin, "and, yet, to do you credit, you have thrown a strong light on a very mysterious subject. Not a magistrate, not a special reporter, who has been engaged on this case, has come so near the truth. It is a marvellous display of intuition and logic."

"Oh! A person has simply to use his brains," said Herlock Sholmes, nattered at the homage of the expert criminal.

"And so few have any brains to use," replied Lupin. "And, now, that the field of conjectures has been narrowed down, and the rubbish cleared away—"

"Well, now, I have simply to discover why the three episodes were enacted at 25 rue Clapeyron, 134 avenue Henri-Martin, and within the walls of the Château de Crozon and my work will be finished. What remains will be child's play. Don't you think so?"

"Yes, I think you are right."

"In that case, Monsieur Lupin, am I wrong in saying that my business will be finished in ten days?"

"In ten days you will know the whole truth," said Lupin.

"And you will be arrested."

"No."

"No?"

"In order that I may be arrested there must occur such a series of improbable and unexpected misfortunes that I cannot admit the possibility of such an event."

"We have a saying in England that 'the unexpected always happens'."

They looked at each other for a moment calmly and fearlessly, without any display of bravado or malice. They met as equals in a contest of wit and skill. And this meeting was the formal crossing of swords, preliminary to the duel.

"Ah!" exclaimed Lupin, "at last I shall have an adversary worthy of the name—one whose defeat will be the proudest achievement in my career."

"Are you not afraid!" asked Wilson.

"Almost, Monsieur Wilson," replied Lupin, rising from his chair, "and the proof is that I am about to make a hasty retreat. Then, we will say ten days, Monsieur Sholmes?"

"Yes, ten days. This is Sunday. A week from next Wednesday, at eight o'clock in the evening, it will be all over."

"And I shall be in prison?"

"No doubt of it."

"Ha! Not a pleasant outlook for a man who gets so much enjoyment out of life as I do. No cares, a lively interest in the affairs of the world, a justifiable contempt for the police, and the consoling sympathy of numerous friends and admirers. And now, behold, all that is about to be changed! It is the reverse side of the medal. After sunshine comes the rain. It is no longer a laughing matter. Adieu!"

"Hurry up!" said Wilson, full of solicitude for a person in whom Herlock Sholmes had inspired so much respect, "do not lose a minute."

"Not a minute, Monsieur Wilson; but I wish to express my pleasure at having met you, and to tell you how much I envy the master in having such a valuable assistant as you seem to be."

Then, after they had courteously saluted each other, like adversaries in a duel who entertain no feeling of malice but are obliged to fight by force of circumstances, Lupin seized me by the arm and drew me outside.

"What do you think of it, dear boy? The strange events of this evening will form an interesting chapter in the memoirs you are now preparing for me."

He closed the door of the restaurant behind us, and, after taking a few steps, he stopped and said:

"Do you smoke?"

"No. Nor do you, it seems to me."

"You are right, I don't."

He lighted a cigarette with a wax-match, which he shook several times in an effort to extinguish it. But he threw away the cigarette immediately, ran across the street, and joined two men who emerged from the shadows as if called by a signal. He conversed with them for a few minutes on the opposite sidewalk, and then returned to me.

"I beg your pardon, but I fear that cursed Sholmes is going to give me trouble. But, I assure you, he is not yet through with Arsène Lupin. He will find out what kind of fuel I use to warm my blood. And now—au revoir! The genial Wilson is right; there is not a moment to lose."

He walked away rapidly.

Thus ended the events of that exciting evening, or, at least, that part of them in which I was a participant. Subsequently, during the course of the evening, other stirring incidents occurred which have come to my knowledge through the courtesy of other members of that unique dinner-party.

At the very moment in which Lupin left me, Herlock Sholmes rose from the table, and looked at his watch.

"Twenty minutes to nine. At nine o'clock I am to meet the Count and Countess at the railway station."

"Then, we must be off!" exclaimed Wilson, between two drinks of whisky.

They left the restaurant.

"Wilson, don't look behind. We may be followed, and, in that case, let us act as if we did not care. Wilson, I want your opinion: why was Lupin in that restaurant?"

"To get something to eat," replied Wilson, quickly.

"Wilson, I must congratulate you on the accuracy of your deduction. I couldn't have done better myself."

Wilson blushed with pleasure, and Sholmes continued:

"To get something to eat. Very well, and, after that, probably, to assure himself whether I am going to the Château de Crozon, as announced by Ganimard in his interview. I must go in order not to disappoint him. But, in order to gain time on him, I shall not go."

"Ah!" said Wilson, nonplussed.

"You, my friend, will walk down this street, take a carriage, two, three carriages. Return later and get the valises that we left at the station, and make for the Elysée-Palace at a gallop."

"And when I reach the Elysée-Palace?"

"Engage a room, go to sleep, and await my orders."

Quite proud of the important rôle assigned to him, Wilson set out to perform his task. Herlock Sholmes proceeded to the railway station, bought a ticket, and repaired to the Amiens' express in which the Count and Countess de Crozon were already installed. He bowed to them, lighted his pipe, and had a quiet smoke in the corridor. The train started. Ten minutes later he took a seat beside the Countess, and said to her:

"Have you the ring here, madame?"

"Yes."

"Will you kindly let me see it?"

He took it, and examined it closely.

"Just as I suspected: it is a manufactured diamond."

"A manufactured diamond?"

"Yes; a new process which consists in submitting diamond dust to a tremendous heat until it melts and is then moulded into a single stone."

"But my diamond is genuine."

"Yes, *your* diamond is; but this is not yours."

"Where is mine?"

"It is held by Arsène Lupin."

"And this stone?"

"Was substituted for yours, and slipped into Herr Bleichen's tooth-powder, where it was afterwards found."

"Then you think this is false?"

"Absolutely false."

The Countess was overwhelmed with surprise and grief, while her husband scrutinized the diamond with an incredulous air. Finally she stammered:

"Is it possible? And why did they not merely steal it and be done with it? And how did they steal it?"

"That is exactly what I am going to find out."

"At the Château de Crozon?"

"No. I shall leave the train at Creil and return to Paris. It is there the game between me and Arsène Lupin must be played. In fact, the game has commenced already, and Lupin thinks I am on my way to the château."

"But—"

"What does it matter to you, madame? The essential thing is your diamond, is it not?"

"Yes."

"Well, don't worry. I have just undertaken a much more difficult task than that. You have my promise that I will restore the true diamond to you within ten days."

The train slackened its speed. He put the false diamond in his pocket and opened the door. The Count cried out:

"That is the wrong side of the train. You are getting out on the tracks."

"That is my intention. If Lupin has anyone on my track, he will lose sight of me now. Adieu."

An employee protested in vain. After the departure of the train, the Englishman sought the station-master's office. Forty minutes later he leaped into a train that landed him in Paris shortly before midnight. He ran across the platform, entered the lunch-room, made his exit at another door, and jumped into a cab.

"Driver—rue Clapeyron."

Having reached the conclusion that he was not followed, he stopped the carriage at the end of the street, and proceeded to make a careful examination of Monsieur Detinan's house and the two adjoining houses. He made measurements of certain distances and entered the figures in his notebook.

"Driver—avenue Henri-Martin."

At the corner of the avenue and the rue de la Pompe, he dismissed the carriage, walked down the street to number 134, and performed the same operations in front of the house of the late Baron d'Hautrec and the two adjoining houses, measuring the width of the respective façades and calculating the depth of the little gardens that stood in front of them.

The avenue was deserted, and was very dark under its four rows of trees, between which, at considerable intervals, a few gas-lamps struggled in vain to light the deep shadows. One of them threw a dim light over a portion of the house, and Sholmes perceived the "To-let" sign posted on the gate, the neglected walks which encircled the small lawn, and the large bare windows of the vacant house.

"I suppose," he said to himself, "the house has been unoccupied since the death of the baron... Ah! if I could only get in and view the scene of the murder!"

No sooner did the idea occur to him than he sought to put it in execution. But how could he manage it? He could not climb over the gate; it was too high. So he took from his pocket an electric lantern and a skeleton key which he always carried. Then, to his great surprise, he discovered that the gate was not locked; in fact, it was open about three or four inches. He entered the garden, and was careful to leave the gate as he had found it—partly open. But he had not taken many steps from the gate when he stopped. He had seen a light pass one of the windows on the second floor.

He saw the light pass a second window and a third, but he saw nothing else, except a silhouette outlined on the walls of the rooms. The light descended to the first floor, and, for a long time, wandered from room to room.

"Who the deuce is walking, at one o'clock in the morning, through the house in which the Baron d'Hautrec was killed?" Herlock Sholmes asked himself, deeply interested.

There was only one way to find out, and that was to enter the house himself. He did not hesitate, but started for the door of the house. However, at the moment when he crossed the streak of gaslight that came from the street-lamp, the man must have seen him, for the light in the house was suddenly extinguished and Herlock Sholmes did not see it again. Softly, he tried the door. It was open, also. Hearing no sound, he advanced through the hallway, encountered the foot of the stairs, and ascended to the first floor. Here there was the same silence, the same darkness.

He entered, one of the rooms and approached a window through which came a feeble light from the outside. On looking through the window he saw the man, who had no doubt descended by another stairway and escaped by another door. The man was threading his way through the shrubbery which bordered the wall that separated the two gardens.

"The deuce!" exclaimed Sholmes, "he is going to escape."

He hastened down the stairs and leaped over the steps in his eagerness to cut off the man's retreat. But he did not see anyone, and, owing to the darkness, it was several seconds before he was able to distinguish a bulky form moving through the shrubbery. This gave the Englishman food for reflection. Why had the man not made his escape, which he could have done so easily? Had he remained in order to watch the movements of the intruder who had disturbed him in his mysterious work?

"At all events," concluded Sholmes, "it is not Lupin; he would be more adroit. It may be one of his men."

For several minutes Herlock Sholmes remained motionless, with his gaze fixed on the adversary who, in his turn was watching the detective. But as that adversary had become passive, and as the Englishman was not one to consume his time in idle waiting, he examined his revolver to see if it was in good working order, remove his knife from its sheath, and walked toward the enemy with that cool effrontery and scorn of danger for which he had become famous.

He heard a clicking sound; it was his adversary preparing his revolver. Herlock Sholmes dashed boldly into the thicket, and grappled with his foe. There was a sharp, desperate struggle, in the course of which Sholmes suspected that the man was trying to draw a knife. But the Englishman, believing his antagonist to be an accomplice of Arsène Lupin and anxious to win the first trick in the game with that redoubtable foe, fought with unusual strength and determination. He hurled his adversary to the ground, held him there with the weight of his body, and, gripping him by the throat with one hand, he used his free hand to take out his electric lantern, press the button, and throw the light over the face of his prisoner.

"Wilson!" he exclaimed, in amazement.

"Herlock Sholmes!" stammered a weak, stifled voice.

For a long time they remained silent, astounded, foolish. The shriek of an automobile rent the air. A slight breeze stirred the leaves. Suddenly, Herlock Sholmes seized his friend by the shoulders and shook him violently, as he cried:

"What are you doing here? Tell me... What?... Did I tell you to hide in the bushes and spy on me?"

"Spy on you!" muttered Wilson, "why, I didn't know it was you."

"But what are you doing here? You ought to be in bed."

"I was in bed."

"You ought to be asleep."

"I was asleep."

"Well, what brought you here?" asked Sholmes.

"Your letter."

"My letter? I don't understand."

"Yes, a messenger brought it to me at the hotel."

"From me? Are you crazy?"

"It is true—I swear it."

"Where is the letter?"

Wilson handed him a sheet of paper, which he read by the light of his lantern. It was as follows:

"Wilson, come at once to avenue Henri-Martin. The house is empty. Inspect the whole place and make an exact plan. Then return to hotel.—Herlock Sholmes."

"I was measuring the rooms," said Wilson, "when I saw a shadow in the garden. I had only one idea——"

"That was to seize the shadow... The idea was excellent... But remember this, Wilson, whenever you receive a letter from me, be sure it is my handwriting and not a forgery."

"Ah!" exclaimed Wilson, as the truth dawned on him, "then the letter wasn't from you?"

"No."

"Who sent it, then?"

"Arsène Lupin."

"Why? For what purpose?" asked Wilson.

"I don't know, and that's what worries me. I don't understand why he took the trouble to disturb you. Of course, if he had sent me on such a foolish errand I wouldn't be surprised; but what was his object in disturbing you?"

"I must hurry back to the hotel."

"So must I, Wilson."

They arrived at the gate. Wilson, who was ahead, took hold of it and pulled.

"Ah! You closed it?" he said.

"No, I left it partly open."

Sholmes tried the gate; then, alarmed, he examined the lock. An oath escaped him:

"Good God! it is locked! locked with a key!"

He shook the gate with all his strength; then, realizing the futility of his efforts, he dropped his arms, discouraged, and muttered, in a jerky manner:

"I can see it all now—it is Lupin. He fore-saw that I would leave the train at Creil, and he prepared this neat little trap for me in case I should commence my investigation this evening. Moreover, he was kind enough to send me a companion to share my captivity. All done to make me lose a day, and, perhaps, also, to teach me to mind my own business."

"Do you mean to say we are prisoners?"

"Exactly. Herlock Sholmes and Wilson are the prisoners of Arsène Lupin. It's a bad beginning; but he laughs best who laughs last."

Wilson seized Sholmes' arm, and exclaimed:

"Look!... Look up there!... A light..."

A light shone through one of the windows of the first floor. Both of them ran to the house, and each ascended by the stairs he had used on coming out a short time before, and they met again at the entrance to the lighted chamber. A small piece of a candle was burning in the centre of the room. Beside it there was a basket containing a bottle, a roasted chicken, and a loaf of bread.

Sholmes was greatly amused, and laughed heartily.

"Wonderful! We are invited to supper. It is really an enchanted place, a genuine fairy-land. Come, Wilson, cheer up! This is not a funeral. It's all very funny."

"Are you quite sure it is so very funny?" asked Wilson, in a lugubrious tone.

"Am I sure?" exclaimed Sholmes, with a gaiety that was too boisterous to be natural, "why, to tell the truth, it's the funniest thing I ever saw. It's a jolly good comedy! What a master of sarcasm this Arsène Lupin is! He makes a fool of you with the utmost grace and delicacy. I wouldn't miss this feast for all the money in the Bank of England. Come, Wilson, you grieve me.

You should display that nobility of character which rises superior to misfortune. I don't see that you have any cause for complaint, really, I don't."

After a time, by dint of good humour and sarcasm, he managed to restore Wilson to his normal mood, and make him swallow a morsel of chicken and a glass of wine. But when the candle went out and they prepared to spend the night there, with the bare floor for a mattress and the hard wall for a pillow, the harsh and ridiculous side of the situation was impressed upon them. That particular incident will not form a pleasant page in the memoirs of the famous detective.

Next morning Wilson awoke, stiff and cold. A slight noise attracted his attention: Herlock Sholmes was kneeling on the floor, critically examining some grains of sand and studying some chalk-marks, now almost effaced, which formed certain figures and numbers, which figures he entered in his notebook.

Accompanied by Wilson, who was deeply interested in the work, he examined each room, and found similar chalk-marks in two other apartments. He noticed, also, two circles on the oaken panels, an arrow on a wainscot, and four figures on four steps of the stairs. At the end of an hour Wilson said:

"The figures are correct, aren't they?"

"I don't know; but, at all events, they mean something," replied Sholmes, who had forgotten the discomforts of the night in the joy created by his new discoveries.

"It is quite obvious," said Wilson, "they represent the number of pieces in the floor."

"Ah!"

"Yes. And the two circles indicate that the panels are false, as you can readily ascertain, and the arrow points in the direction in which the panels move."

Herlock Sholmes looked at Wilson, in astonishment.

"Ah! my dear friend, how do you know all that? Your clairvoyance makes my poor ability in that direction look quite insignificant."

"Oh! it is very simple," said Wilson, inflated with pride; "I examined those marks last night, according to your instructions, or, rather, according to the instructions of Arsène Lupin, since he wrote the letter you sent to me."

At that moment Wilson faced a greater danger than he had during his struggle in the garden with Herlock Sholmes. The latter now felt a furious desire to strangle him. But, dominating his feelings, Sholmes made a grimace which was intended for a smile, and said:

"Quite so, Wilson, you have done well, and your work shows commendable progress. But, tell me, have you exercised your powers of observation and analysis on any other points? I might profit by your deductions."

"Oh! No, I went no farther."

"That's a pity. Your début was such a promising one. But, since that is all, we may as well go."

"Go! But how can we get out?"

"The way all honest people go out: through the gate."

"But it is locked."

"It will be opened."

"By whom?"

"Please call the two policemen who are strolling down the avenue."

"But——"

"But what?"

"It is very humiliating. What will be said when it becomes known that Herlock Sholmes and Wilson were the prisoners of Arsène Lupin?"

"Of course, I understand they will roar with laughter," replied Herlock Sholmes, in a dry voice and with frowning features, "but we can't set up housekeeping in this place."

"And you will not try to find another way out?"

"No."

"But the man who brought us the basket of provisions did not cross the garden, coming or going. There is some other way out. Let us look for it, and not bother with the police."

"Your argument is sound, but you forget that all the detectives in Paris have been trying to find it for the last six months, and that I searched the house from top to bottom while you were asleep. Ah! My dear Wilson, we have not been accustomed to pursue such game as Arsène Lupin. He leaves no trail behind him."

At eleven o'clock, Herlock Sholmes and Wilson were liberated, and conducted to the nearest police station, where the commissary, after subjecting them to a severe examination, released them with an affectation of good-will that was quite exasperating.

"I am very sorry, messieurs, that this unfortunate incident has occurred. You will have a very poor opinion of French hospitality. Mon Dieu! What a night you must have passed! Ah! that rascally Lupin is no respecter of persons."

They took a carriage to their hotel. At the office Wilson asked for the key of his room.

After some search the clerk replied, much astonished:

"But, monsieur, you have given up the room."

"I gave it up? When?"

"This morning, by the letter your friend brought here."

"What friend?"

"The gentleman who brought your letter... Ah! your card is still attached to the letter. Here they are."

Wilson looked at them. Certainly, it was one of his cards, and the letter was in his handwriting.

"Good Lord!" he muttered, "this is another of his tricks," and he added, aloud: "Where is my luggage?"

"Your friend took it."

"Ah!... and you gave it to him?"

"Certainly; on the strength of your letter and card."

"Of course... of course."

They left the hotel and walked, slowly and thoughtfully, through the Champs-Elysées. The avenue was bright and cheerful beneath a clear autumn sun; the air was mild and pleasant.

At Rond-Point, Herlock Sholmes lighted his pipe. Then Wilson spoke:

"I can't understand you, Sholmes. You are so calm and unruffled. They play with you as a cat plays with a mouse, and yet you do not say a word."

Sholmes stopped, as he replied:

"Wilson, I was thinking of your card."

"Well?"

"The point is this: here is a man who, in view of a possible struggle with us, procures specimens of our handwriting, and who holds, in his possession, one or more of your cards. Now, have you considered how much precaution and skill those facts represent?"

"Well?"

"Well, Wilson, to overcome an enemy so well prepared and so thoroughly equipped requires the infinite shrewdness of ... of a Herlock Sholmes. And yet, as you have seen, Wilson, I have lost the first round."

At six o'clock the *Echo de France* published the following article in its evening edition:

"This morning Mon. Thenard, commissary of police in the sixteenth district, released Herlock Sholmes and his friend Wilson, both of whom had been locked in the house of the late Baron d'Hautrec, where they spent a very pleasant night—thanks to the thoughtful care and attention of Arsène Lupin."

"In addition to their other troubles, these gentlemen have been robbed of their valises, and, in consequence thereof, they have entered a formal complaint against Arsène Lupin."

"Arsène Lupin, satisfied that he has given them a mild reproof, hopes these gentlemen will not force him to resort to more stringent measures."

"Bah!" exclaimed Herlock Sholmes, crushing the paper in his hands, "that is only child's play! And that is the only criticism I have to make of Arsène Lupin: he plays to the gallery. There is that much of the fakir in him."

"Ah! Sholmes, you are a wonderful man! You have such a command over your temper. Nothing ever disturbs you."

"No, nothing disturbs me," replied Sholmes, in a voice that trembled from rage; "besides, what's the use of losing my temper?... I am quite confident of the final result; I shall have the last word."

Chapter 4

LIGHT IN THE DARKNESS

HOWEVER well-tempered a man's character may be—and Herlock Sholmes is one of those men over whom ill-fortune has little or no hold—there are circumstances wherein the most courageous combatant feels the necessity of marshalling his forces before risking the chances of a battle.

"I shall take a vacation to-day," said Sholmes.

"And what shall I do?" asked Wilson.

"You, Wilson—let me see! You can buy some underwear and linen to replenish our wardrobe, while I take a rest."

"Very well, Sholmes, I will watch while you sleep."

Wilson uttered these words with all the importance of a sentinel on guard at the outpost, and therefore exposed to the greatest danger. His chest was expanded; his muscles were tense. Assuming a shrewd look, he scrutinized, officially, the little room in which they had fixed their abode.

"Very well, Wilson, you can watch. I shall occupy myself in the preparation of a line of attack more appropriate to the methods of the enemy we are called upon to meet. Do you see, Wilson, we have been deceived in this fellow Lupin. My opinion is that we must commence at the very beginning of this affair."

"And even before that, if possible. But have we sufficient time?"

"Nine days, dear boy. That is five too many."

The Englishman spent the entire afternoon in smoking and sleeping. He did not enter upon his new plan of attack until the following day. Then he said:

"Wilson, I am ready. Let us attack the enemy."

"Lead on, Macduff!" exclaimed Wilson, full of martial ardour. "I wish to fight in the front rank. Oh! have no fear. I shall do credit to my King and country, for I am an Englishman."

In the first place, Sholmes had three long and important interviews: With Monsieur Detinan, whose rooms he examined with the greatest care and precision; with Suzanne Gerbois, whom he questioned in regard to the blonde Lady; and with Sister Auguste, who had retired to the convent of the Visitandines since the murder of Baron d'Hautrec.

At each of these interviews Wilson had remained outside; and each time he asked:

"Satisfactory?"

"Quite so."

"I was sure we were on the right track."

They paid a visit to the two houses adjoining that of the late Baron d'Hautrec in the avenue Henri-Martin; then they visited the rue Clapeyron, and, while he was examining the front of number 25, Sholmes said:

"All these houses must be connected by secret passages, but I can't find them."

For the first time in his life, Wilson doubted the omnipotence of his famous associate. Why did he now talk so much and accomplish so little?

"Why?" exclaimed Sholmes, in answer to Wilson's secret thought, "because, with this fellow Lupin, a person has to work in the dark, and, instead of deducting the truth from established facts, a man must extract it from his own brain, and afterward learn if it is supported by the facts in the case."

"But what about the secret passages?"

"They must exist. But even though I should discover them, and thus learn how Arsène Lupin made his entrance to the lawyer's house and how the blonde Lady escaped from the house of Baron d'Hautrec after the murder, what good would it do? How would it help me? Would it furnish me with a weapon of attack?"

"Let us attack him just the same," exclaimed Wilson, who had scarcely uttered these words when he jumped back with a cry of alarm. Something had fallen at their feet; it was a bag filled with sand which might have caused them serious injury if it had struck them.

Sholmes looked up. Some men were working on a scaffolding attached to the balcony at the fifth floor of the house. He said:

"We were lucky; one step more, and that heavy bag would have fallen on our heads. I wonder if—"

Moved by a sudden impulse, he rushed into the house, up the five flights of stairs, rang the bell, pushed his way into the apartment to the great surprise and alarm of the servant who came to the door, and made his way to the balcony in front of the house. But there was no one there.

"Where are the workmen who were here a moment ago?" he asked the servant.

"They have just gone."

"Which way did they go?"

"By the servants' stairs."

Sholmes leaned out of the window. He saw two men leaving the house, carrying bicycles. They mounted them and quickly disappeared around the corner.

"How long have they been working on this scaffolding?"

"Those men?... Only since this morning. It's their first day."

Sholmes returned to the street, and joined Wilson. Together they returned to the hotel, and thus the second day ended in a mournful silence.

On the following day their programme was almost similar. They sat together on a bench in the avenue Henri-Martin, much to Wilson's disgust, who did not find it amusing to spend long hours watching the house in which the tragedy had occurred.

"What do you expect, Sholmes? That Arsène Lupin will walk out of the house?"

"No."

"That the blonde Lady will make her appearance?"

"No."

"What then?"

"I am looking for something to occur; some slight incident that will furnish me with a clue to work on."

"And if it does not occur!"

"Then I must, myself, create the spark that will set fire to the powder."

A solitary incident—and that of a disagreeable nature—broke the monotony of the forenoon.

A gentleman was riding along the avenue when his horse suddenly turned aside in such a manner that it ran against the bench on which they were sitting, and struck Sholmes a slight blow on the shoulder.

"Ha!" exclaimed Sholmes, "a little more and I would have had a broken shoulder."

The gentleman struggled with his horse. The Englishman drew his revolver and pointed it; but Wilson seized his arm, and said:

"Don't be foolish! What are you going to do! Kill the man!"

"Leave me alone, Wilson! Let go!"

During the brief struggle between Sholmes and Wilson the stranger rode away.

"Now, you can shoot," said Wilson, triumphantly, when the horseman was at some distance.

"Wilson, you're an idiot! Don't you understand that the man is an accomplice of Arsène Lupin?"

Sholmes was trembling from rage. Wilson stammered pitifully:

"What!... that man... an accomplice?"

"Yes, the same as the workmen who tried to drop the bag of sand on us yesterday."

"It can't be possible!"

"Possible or not, there was only one way to prove it."

"By killing the man?"

"No—by killing the horse. If you hadn't grabbed my arm, I should have captured one of Lupin's accomplices. Now, do you understand the folly of your act?"

Throughout the afternoon both men were morose. They did not speak a word to each other. At five o'clock they visited the rue Clapeyron, but were careful to keep at a safe distance from the houses. However, three young men who were passing through the street, arm in arm, singing, ran against Sholmes and Wilson and refused to let them pass. Sholmes, who was in an ill humour, contested the right of way with them. After a brief struggle, Sholmes resorted to his fists. He struck one of the men a hard blow on the chest, another a blow in the face, and thus subdued two of his adversaries. Thereupon the three of them took to their heels and disappeared.

"Ah!" exclaimed Sholmes, "that does me good. I needed a little exercise."

But Wilson was leaning against the wall. Sholmes said:

"What's the matter, old chap? You're quite pale."

Wilson pointed to his left arm, which hung inert, and stammered:

"I don't know what it is. My arm pains me."

"Very much?... Is it serious?"

"Yes, I am afraid so."

He tried to raise his arm, but it was helpless. Sholmes felt it, gently at first, then in a rougher way, "to see how badly it was hurt," he said. He concluded that Wilson was really hurt, so he led him to a neighboring pharmacy, where a closer examination revealed the fact that the arm was broken and that Wilson was a candidate for the hospital. In the meantime they bared his arm and applied some remedies to ease his suffering.

"Come, come, old chap, cheer up!" said Sholmes, who was holding Wilson's arm, "in five or six weeks you will be all right again. But I will pay them back... the rascals! Especially Lupin, for this is his work... no doubt of that. I swear to you if ever—"

He stopped suddenly, dropped the arm—which caused Wilson such an access of pain that he almost fainted—and, striking his forehead, Sholmes said:

"Wilson, I have an idea. You know, I have one occasionally."

He stood for a moment, silent, with staring eyes, and then muttered, in short, sharp phrases:

"Yes, that's it... that will explain all... right at my feet... and I didn't see it... ah, parbleu! I should have thought of it before... Wilson, I shall have good news for you."

Abruptly leaving his old friend, Sholmes ran into the street and went directly to the house known as number 25. On one of the stones, to the right of the door, he read this inscription: "Destange, architect, 1875."

There was a similar inscription on the house numbered 23.

Of course, there was nothing unusual in that. But what might be read on the houses in the avenue Henri-Martin?

A carriage was passing. He engaged it and directed the driver to take him to No. 134 avenue Henri-Martin. He was roused to a high pitch of excitement. He stood up in the carriage and urged the horse to greater speed. He offered extra pourboires to the driver. Quicker! Quicker!

How great was his anxiety as they turned from the rue de la Pompe! Had he caught a glimpse of the truth at last?

On one of the stones of the late Baron's house he read the words: "Destange, architect, 1874." And a similar inscription appeared on the two adjoining houses.

The reaction was such that he settled down in the seat of the carriage, trembling from joy. At last, a tiny ray of light had penetrated the dark shadows which encompassed these mysterious crimes! In the vast sombre forest wherein a thousand pathways crossed and re-crossed, he had discovered the first clue to the track followed by the enemy!

He entered a branch post office and obtained telephonic connection with the château de Crozon. The Countess answered the telephone call.

"Hello!... Is that you, madame?"

"Monsieur Sholmes, isn't it? Everything going all right?"

"Quite well, but I wish to ask you one question... Hello!"

"Yes, I hear you."

"Tell me, when was the château de Crozon built?"

"It was destroyed by fire and rebuilt about thirty years ago."

"Who built it, and in what year?"

"There is an inscription on the front of the house which reads: 'Lucien Destange, architect, 1877.'"

"Thank you, madame, that is all. Good-bye."

He went away, murmuring: "Destange ... Lucien Destange ... that name has a familiar sound."

He noticed a public reading-room, entered, consulted a dictionary of modern biography, and copied the following information: "Lucien Destange, born 1840, Grand-Prix de Rome, officer of the Legion of Honour, author of several valuable books on architecture, etc..."

Then he returned to the pharmacy and found that Wilson had been taken to the hospital. There Sholmes found him with his arm in splints, and shivering with fever.

"Victory! Victory!" cried Sholmes. "I hold one end of the thread."

"Of what thread?"

"The one that leads to victory. I shall now be walking on solid ground, where there will be footprints, clues..."

"Cigarette ashes?" asked Wilson, whose curiosity had overcome his pain.

"And many other things! Just think, Wilson, I have found the mysterious link which unites the different adventures in which the blonde Lady played a part. Why did Lupin select those three houses for the scenes of his exploits?"

"Yes, why?"

"Because those three houses were built by the same architect. That was an easy problem, eh? Of course... but who would have thought of it?"

"No one but you."

"And who, except I, knows that the same architect, by the use of analogous plans, has rendered it possible for a person to execute three distinct acts which, though miraculous in appearance, are, in reality, quite simple and easy?"

"That was a stroke of good luck."

"And it was time, dear boy, as I was becoming very impatient. You know, this is our fourth day."

"Out of ten."

"Oh! after this—"

Sholmes was excited, delighted, and gayer than usual.

"And when I think that these rascals might have attacked me in the street and broken my arm just as they did yours! Isn't that so, Wilson?"

Wilson simply shivered at the horrible thought. Sholmes continued:

"We must profit by the lesson. I can see, Wilson, that we were wrong to try and fight Lupin in the open, and leave ourselves exposed to his attacks."

"I can see it, and feel it, too, in my broken arm," said Wilson.

"You have one consolation, Wilson; that is, that I escaped. Now, I must be doubly cautious. In an open fight he will defeat me; but if I can work in the dark, unseen by him, I have the advantage, no matter how strong his forces may be."

"Ganimard might be of some assistance."

"Never! On the day that I can truly say: Arsène Lupin is there; I show you the quarry, and how to catch it; I shall go and see Ganimard at one of the two addresses that he gave me—his residence in the rue Pergolese, or at the Suisse tavern in the Place du Châtelet. But, until that time, I shall work alone."

He approached the bed, placed his hand on Wilson's shoulder—on the sore one, of course—and said to him:

"Take care of yourself, old fellow. Henceforth your role will be to keep two or three of Arsène Lupin's men busy watching here in vain for my return to enquire about your health. It is a secret mission for you, eh?"

"Yes, and I shall do my best to fulfil it conscientiously. Then you do not expect to come here anymore?"

"What for?" asked Sholmes.

"I don't know... of course... I am getting on as well as possible. But, Herlock, do me a last service: give me a drink."

"A drink?"

"Yes, I am dying of thirst; and with my fever—"

"To be sure—directly—"

He made a pretence of getting some water, perceived a package of tobacco, lighted his pipe, and then, as if he had not heard his friend's request, he went away, whilst Wilson uttered a mute prayer for the inaccessible water.

"Monsieur Destange!"

The servant eyed from head to foot the person to whom he had opened the door of the house—the magnificent house that stood at the corner of the Place Malesherbes and the rue Montchanin—and at the sight of the man with gray hairs, badly shaved, dressed in a shabby black coat, with a body as ill-formed and ungracious as his face, he replied with the disdain which he thought the occasion warranted:

"Monsieur Destange may or may not be at home. That depends. Has monsieur a card?"

Monsieur did not have a card, but he had a letter of introduction and, after the servant had taken the letter to Mon. Destange, he was conducted into the presence of that gentleman who was sitting in a large circular room or rotunda which occupied one of the wings of the house. It was a library, and contained a profusion of books and architectural drawings. When the stranger entered, the architect said to him:

"You are Monsieur Stickmann?"

"Yes, monsieur."

"My secretary tells me that he is ill, and has sent you to continue the general catalogue of the books which he commenced under my direction, and, more particularly, the catalogue of German books. Are you familiar with that kind of work?"

"Yes, monsieur, quite so," he replied, with a strong German accent.

Under those circumstances the bargain was soon concluded, and Mon. Destange commenced work with his new secretary.

Herlock Sholmes had gained access to the house.

In order to escape the vigilance of Arsène Lupin and gain admittance to the house occupied by Lucien Destange and his daughter Clotilde, the famous detective had been compelled to resort to a number of stratagems, and, under a variety of names, to ingratiate himself into the good graces and confidence of a number of persons—in short, to live, during forty-eight hours, a most complicated life. During that time he had acquired the following information: Mon. Destange, having retired from active business on account of his failing health, now lived amongst the many books he had accumulated on the subject of architecture. He derived infinite pleasure in viewing and handling those dusty old volumes.

His daughter Clotilde was considered eccentric. She passed her time in another part of the house, and never went out.

"Of course," Sholmes said to himself, as he wrote in a register the titles of the books which Mon. Destange dictated to him, "all that is vague and incomplete, but it is quite a long step in advance. I shall surely solve one of these absorbing problems: Is Mon. Destange associated with Arsène Lupin? Does he continue to see him? Are the papers relating to the construction of the three houses still in existence? Will those papers not furnish me with the location of other houses of similar construction which Arsène Lupin and his associates will plunder in the future?

"Monsieur Destange, an accomplice of Arsène Lupin! That venerable man, an officer of the Legion of Honor, working in league with a burglar—such an idea was absurd! Besides, if we concede that such a complicity exists, how could Mon. Destange, thirty years ago, have possibly foreseen the thefts of Arsène Lupin, who was then an infant?"

No matter! The Englishman was implacable. With his marvellous scent, and that instinct which never fails him, he felt that he was in the heart of some strange mystery. Ever since he first entered the house, he had been under the influence of that impression, and yet he could not define the grounds on which he based his suspicions.

Up to the morning of the second day he had not made any significant discovery. At two o'clock of that day he saw Clotilde Destange for the first time; she came to the library in search of a book. She was about thirty years of age, a brunette, slow and silent in her movements, with features imbued with that expression of indifference which is characteristic of people who live a secluded life. She exchanged a few words with her father, and then retired, without even looking at Sholmes.

The afternoon dragged along monotonously. At five o'clock Mon. Destange announced his intention to go out. Sholmes was alone on the circular gallery that was constructed about ten feet above the floor of the rotunda. It was almost dark. He was on the point of going out, when he heard a slight sound and, at the same time, experienced the feeling that there was someone in the room. Several minutes passed before he saw or heard anything more. Then he shuddered; a shadowy form emerged from the gloom, quite close to him, upon the balcony. It seemed incredible. How long had this mysterious visitor been there? Whence did he come?

The strange man descended the steps and went directly to a large oaken cupboard. Sholmes was a keen observer of the man's movements. He watched him searching amongst the papers with which the cupboard was filled. What was he looking for?

Then the door opened and Mlle. Destange entered, speaking to someone who was following her:

"So you have decided not to go out, father?... Then I will make a light... one second... do not move..."

The strange man closed the cupboard and hid in the embrasure of a large window, drawing the curtains together. Did Mlle. Destange not see him? Did she not hear him? Calmly she turned on the electric lights; she and her father sat down close to each other. She opened a book she had brought with her, and commenced to read. After the lapse of a few minutes she said:

"Your secretary has gone."

"Yes, I don't see him."

"Do you like him as well as you did at first?" she asked, as if she were not aware of the illness of the real secretary and his replacement by Stickmann.

"Oh! Yes."

Monsieur Destange's head bobbed from one side to the other. He was asleep. The girl resumed her reading. A moment later one of the window curtains was pushed back, and the strange man emerged and glided along the wall toward the door, which obliged him to pass behind Mon. Destange but in front of Clotilde, and brought him into the light so that Herlock Sholmes obtained a good view of the man's face. It was Arsène Lupin.

The Englishman was delighted. His forecast was verified; he had penetrated to the very heart of the mystery, and found Arsène Lupin to be the moving spirit in it.

Clotilde had not yet displayed any knowledge of his presence, although it was quite improbable that any movement of the intruder had escaped her notice. Lupin had almost reached the door and, in fact, his hand was already seeking the door-knob, when his coat brushed against a small table and knocked something to the floor. Monsieur Destange awoke with a start. Arsène Lupin was already standing in front of him, hat in hand, smiling.

"Maxime Bermond," exclaimed Mon. Destange, joyfully. "My dear Maxime, what lucky chance brings you here?"

"The wish to see you and Mademoiselle Destange."

"When did you return from your journey?"

"Yesterday."

"You must stay to dinner."

"No, thank you, I am sorry, but I have an appointment to dine with some friends at a restaurant."

"Come, tomorrow, then, Clotilde, you must urge him to come tomorrow. Ah! My dear Maxime... I thought of you many times during your absence."

"Really?"

"Yes, I went through all my old papers in that cupboard, and found our last statement of account."

"What account?"

"Relating to the avenue Henri-Martin."

"Ah! Do you keep such papers? What for?"

Then the three of them left the room, and continued their conversation in a small parlour which adjoined the library.

"Is it Lupin?" Sholmes asked himself, in a sudden access of doubt. Certainly, from all appearances, it was he; and yet it was also someone else who resembled Arsène Lupin in certain respects, and who still maintained his own individuality, features, and colour of hair. Sholmes could hear Lupin's voice in the adjoining room. He was relating some stories at which Mon. Destange laughed heartily, and which even brought a smile to the lips of the melancholy Clotilde. And each of those smiles appeared to be the reward which Arsène Lupin was seeking, and which he was delighted to have secured. His success caused him to redouble his efforts and, insensibly, at the sound of that clear and happy voice, Clotilde's face brightened and lost that cold and listless expression which usually pervaded it.

"They love each other," thought Sholmes, "but what the deuce can there be in common between Clotilde Destange and Maxime Bermond? Does she know that Maxime is none other than Arsène Lupin?"

Until seven o'clock Sholmes was an anxious listener, seeking to profit by the conversation. Then, with infinite precaution, he descended from the gallery, crept along the side of the room to the door in such a manner that the people in the adjoining room did not see him.

When he reached the street Sholmes satisfied himself that there was neither an automobile nor a cab waiting there; then he slowly limped along the boulevard Malesherbes. He turned into an adjacent street, donned the overcoat which he had carried on his arm, altered the shape of his hat, assumed an upright carriage, and, thus transformed, returned to a place whence he could watch the door of Mon. Destange's house.

In a few minutes Arsène Lupin came out, and proceeded to walk toward the centre of Paris by way of the rues de Constantinople and London. Herlock Sholmes followed at a distance of a hundred paces.

Exciting moments for the Englishman! He sniffed the air, eagerly, like a hound following a fresh scent. It seemed to him a delightful thing thus to follow his adversary. It was no longer Herlock Sholmes who was being watched, but Arsène Lupin, the invisible Arsène Lupin. He held him, so to speak, within the grasp of his eye, by an imperceptible bond that nothing could break. And he was pleased to think that the quarry belonged to him.

But he soon observed a suspicious circumstance. In the intervening space between him and Arsène Lupin he noticed several people traveling in the same direction, particularly two husky fellows in slouch hats on the left side of the street, and two others on the right wearing caps and smoking cigarettes. Of course, their presence in that vicinity may have been the result of chance, but Sholmes was more astonished when he observed that the four men stopped when Lupin entered a tobacco shop; and still more surprised when the four men started again after Lupin emerged from the shop, each keeping to his own side of the street.

"Curse it!" muttered Sholmes; "he is being followed."

He was annoyed at the idea that others were on the trail of Arsène Lupin; that someone might deprive him, not of the glory— he cared little for that—but of the immense pleasure of capturing, single-handed, the most formidable enemy he had ever met. And he felt that he was not mistaken; the men presented to Sholmes' experienced eye the appearance and manner of those who, while regulating their gait to that of another, wish to present a careless and natural air.

"Is this some of Ganimard's work?" muttered Sholmes. "Is he playing me false?"

He felt inclined to speak to one of the men with a view of acting in concert with him; but as they were now approaching the boulevard the crowd was becoming denser, and he was afraid he might lose sight of Lupin. So he quickened his pace and turned into the boulevard just in time to see Lupin ascending the steps of the Hungarian restaurant at the corner of the rue du Helder. The door of the restaurant was open, so that Sholmes, while sitting on a bench on the other side of the boulevard, could see Lupin take a seat at a table, luxuriously appointed and decorated with flowers, at which three gentlemen and two ladies of elegant appearance were already seated and who extended to Lupin a hearty greeting.

Sholmes now looked about for the four men and perceived them amongst a crowd of people who were listening to a gipsy orchestra that was playing in a neighbouring café. It was a curious thing that they were paying no attention to Arsène Lupin, but seemed to be friendly with the people around them. One of them took a cigarette from his pocket and approached a gentleman who wore a frock coat and silk hat. The gentleman offered the other his cigar for a light, and Sholmes had the impression that they talked to each other much longer than the occasion demanded. Finally the gentleman approached the Hungarian restaurant, entered and looked around. When he caught sight of Lupin he advanced and spoke to him for a moment, then took a seat at an adjoining table. Sholmes now recognized this gentleman as the horseman who had tried to run him down in the avenue Henri-Martin.

Then Sholmes understood that these men were not tracking Arsène Lupin; they were a part of his band. They were watching over his safety. They were his bodyguard, his satellites, his vigilant escort. Wherever danger threatened Lupin, these confederates were at hand to avert it, ready to defend him. The four men were accomplices. The gentleman in the frock coat was an accomplice. These facts furnished the Englishman with food for reflection. Would he ever succeed in capturing that inaccessible individual? What unlimited power was possessed by such an organization, directed by such a chief!

He tore a leaf from his notebook, wrote a few lines in pencil, which he placed in an envelope, and said to a boy about fifteen years of age who was sitting on the bench beside him:

"Here, my boy; take a carriage and deliver this letter to the cashier of the Suisse tavern, Place du Châtelet. Be quick!"

He gave him a five-franc piece. The boy disappeared.

A half hour passed away. The crowd had grown larger, and Sholmes perceived only at intervals the accomplices of Arsène Lupin. Then someone brushed against him and whispered in his ear:

"Well? what is it, Monsieur Sholmes?"

"Ah! It is you, Ganimard?"

"Yes; I received your note at the tavern. What's the matter?"

"He is there."

"What do you mean?"

"There... in the restaurant. Lean to the right... Do you see him now?"

"No."

"He is pouring a glass of champagne for the lady."

"That is not Lupin."

"Yes, it is."

"But I tell you... Ah! yet, it may be. It looks a great deal like him," said Ganimard, naively. "And the others—accomplices?"

"No; the lady sitting beside him is Lady Cliveden; the other is the Duchess de Cleath. The gentleman sitting opposite Lupin is the Spanish Ambassador to London."

Ganimard took a step forward. Sholmes retained him.

"Be prudent. You are alone."

"So is he."

"No, he has a number of men on the boulevard mounting guard. And inside the restaurant that gentleman—"

"And I, when I take Arsène Lupin by the collar and announce his name, I shall have the entire room on my side and all the waiters."

"I should prefer to have a few policemen."

"But, Monsieur Sholmes, we have no choice. We must catch him when we can."

He was right; Sholmes knew it. It was better to take advantage of the opportunity and make the attempt. Sholmes simply gave this advice to Ganimard:

"Conceal your identity as long as possible."

Sholmes glided behind a newspaper kiosk, whence he could still watch Lupin, who was leaning toward Lady Cliveden, talking and smiling.

Ganimard crossed the street, hands in his pockets, as if he were going down the boulevard, but when he reached the opposite sidewalk he turned quickly and bounded up the steps of the restaurant. There was a shrill whistle. Ganimard ran against the head waiter, who had suddenly planted himself in the doorway and now pushed Ganimard back with a show of indignation, as if he were an intruder whose presence would bring disgrace upon the restaurant. Ganimard was surprised. At the same moment the gentleman in the frock coat came out. He took the part of the detective and entered into an exciting argument with the waiter; both of them hung on to Ganimard, one pushing him in, the other pushing him out in such a manner that, despite all his efforts and despite his furious protestations, the unfortunate detective soon found himself on the sidewalk.

The struggling men were surrounded by a crowd. Two policemen, attracted by the noise, tried to force their way through the crowd, but encountered a mysterious resistance and could make no headway through the opposing backs and pressing shoulders of the mob.

But suddenly, as if by magic, the crowd parted and the passage to the restaurant was clear. The head waiter, recognizing his mistake, was profuse in his apologies; the gentleman in the frock coat ceased his efforts on behalf of the detective, the crowd dispersed, the policemen passed on, and Ganimard hastened to the table at which the six guests were sitting. But now there were only five! He looked around... The only exit was the door.

"The person who was sitting here!" he cried to the five astonished guests. "Where is he?"

"Monsieur Destro?"

"No; Arsène Lupin!"

A waiter approached and said:

"The gentleman went upstairs."

Ganimard rushed up in the hope of finding him. The upper floor of the restaurant contained private dining-rooms and had a private stairway leading to the boulevard.

"No use looking for him now," muttered Ganimard. "He is far away by this time."

He was not far away—two hundred yards at most—in the Madeleine-Bastille omnibus, which was rolling along very peacefully with its three horses across the Place de l'Opéra toward the Boulevard des Capucines. Two sturdy fellows were talking together on the platform. On the roof of the omnibus near the stairs an old fellow was sleeping; it was Herlock Sholmes.

With bobbing head, rocked by the movement of the vehicle, the Englishman said to himself:

"If Wilson could see me now, how proud he would be of his collaborator!... Bah! It was easy to foresee that the game was lost, as soon as the man whistled; nothing could be done but watch the exits and see that our man did not escape. Really, Lupin makes life exciting and interesting."

At the terminal point Herlock Sholmes, by leaning over, saw Arsène Lupin leaving the omnibus, and as he passed in front of the men who formed his bodyguard Sholmes heard him say: "A l'Etoile."

"A l'Etoile, exactly, a rendezvous. I shall be there," thought Sholmes. "I will follow the two men."

Lupin took an automobile; but the men walked the entire distance, followed by Sholmes. They stopped at a narrow house, No. 40 rue Chalgrin, and rang the bell. Sholmes took his position in the shadow of a doorway, whence he could watch the house in question. A man opened one of the windows of the ground floor and closed the shutters. But the shutters did not reach to the top of the window. The impost was clear.

At the end of ten minutes a gentleman rang at the same door and a few minutes later another man came. A short time afterward an automobile stopped in front of the house, bringing two passengers: Arsène Lupin and a lady concealed beneath a large cloak and a thick veil.

"The blonde Lady, no doubt," said Sholmes to himself, as the automobile drove away.

Herlock Sholmes now approached the house, climbed to the window-ledge and, by standing on tiptoe, he was able to see through the window above the shutters. What did he see?

Arsène Lupin, leaning against the mantel, was speaking with considerable animation. The others were grouped around him, listening to him attentively. Amongst them Sholmes easily recognized the gentleman in the frock coat and he thought one of the other men resembled the head-waiter of the restaurant. As to the blonde Lady, she was seated in an armchair with her back to the window.

"They are holding a consultation," thought Sholmes. "They are worried over the incident at the restaurant and are holding a council of war. Ah! what a master stroke it would be to capture all of them at one fell stroke!"

One of them, having moved toward the door, Sholmes leaped to the ground and concealed himself in the shadow. The gentleman in the frock coat and the head-waiter left the house. A moment later a light appeared at the windows of the first floor, but the shutters were closed immediately and the upper part of the house was dark as well as the lower.

"Lupin and the woman are on the ground floor; the two confederates live on the upper floor," said Sholmes.

Sholmes remained there the greater part of the night, fearing that if he went away Arsène Lupin might leave during his absence. At four o'clock, seeing two policemen at the end of the street, he approached them, explained the situation and left them to watch the house. He went to Ganimard's residence in the rue Pergolese and wakened him.

"I have him yet," said Sholmes.

"Arsène Lupin?"

"Yes."

"If you haven't got any better hold on him than you had a while ago, I might as well go back to bed. But we may as well go to the station-house."

They went to the police station in the rue Mesnil and from there to the residence of the commissary, Mon. Decointre. Then, accompanied by half a dozen policemen, they went to the rue Chalgrin.

"Anything new?" asked Sholmes, addressing the two policemen.

"Nothing."

It was just breaking day when, after taking necessary measures to prevent escape, the commissary rang the bell and commenced to question the concierge. The woman was greatly frightened at this early morning invasion, and she trembled as she replied that there were no tenants on the ground floor.

"What! Not a tenant?" exclaimed Ganimard.

"No; but on the first floor there are two men named Leroux. They have furnished the apartment on the ground floor for some country relations."

"A gentleman and lady."

"Yes."

"Who came here last night."

"Perhaps... but I don't know... I was asleep. But I don't think so, for the key is here. They did not ask for it."

With that key the commissary opened the door of the ground-floor apartment. It comprised only two rooms and they were empty.

"Impossible!" exclaimed Sholmes. "I saw both of them in this room."

"I don't doubt your word," said the commissary; "but they are not here now."

"Let us go to the first floor. They must be there."

"The first floor is occupied by two men named Leroux."

"We will examine the Messieurs Leroux."

They all ascended the stairs and the commissary rang. At the second ring a man opened the door; he was in his shirt-sleeves. Sholmes recognized him as one of Lupin's bodyguard. The man assumed a furious air:

"What do you mean by making such a row at this hour of the morning... waking people up..."

But he stopped suddenly, astounded.

"God forgive me!... really, gentlemen, I didn't notice who it was. Why, it is Monsieur Decointre!... and you, Monsieur Ganimard. What can I do for you!"

Ganimard burst into an uncontrollable fit of laughter, which caused him to bend double and turn black in the face.

"Ah! It is you, Leroux," he stammered. "Oh! This is too funny! Leroux, an accomplice of Arsène Lupin! Oh, I shall die! And your brother, Leroux, where is he?"

"Edmond!" called the man. "It is Ganimard, who has come to visit us."

Another man appeared and at sight of him Ganimard's mirth redoubled.

"Oh! Oh! We had no idea of this! Ah! my friends, you are in a bad fix now. Who would have ever suspected it?"

Turning to Sholmes, Ganimard introduced the man:

"Victor Leroux, a detective from our office, one of the best men in the iron brigade... Edmond Leroux, chief clerk in the anthropometric service."

Chapter 5

AN ABDUCTION

HERLOCK Sholmes said nothing. To protest? To accuse the two men? That would be useless. In the absence of evidence which he did not possess and had no time to seek, no one would believe him. Moreover, he was stifled with rage, but would not display his feelings before the triumphant Ganimard. So he bowed respectfully to the brothers Leroux, guardians of society, and retired.

In the vestibule he turned toward a low door which looked like the entrance to a cellar, and picked up a small red stone; it was a garnet. When he reached the street he turned and read on the front of the house this inscription: "Lucien Destange, architect, 1877."

The adjoining house, No. 42, bore the same inscription.

"Always the double passage—numbers 40 and 42 have a secret means of communication. Why didn't I think of that? I should have remained with the two policemen."

He met the policemen near the corner and said to them:

"Two people came out of house No. 42 during my absence, didn't they?"

"Yes; a gentleman and lady."

Ganimard approached. Sholmes took his arm, and as they walked down the street he said:

"Monsieur Ganimard, you have had a good laugh and will no doubt forgive me for the trouble I have caused you."

"Oh! There's no harm done; but it was a good joke."

"I admit that; but the best jokes have only a short life, and this one can't last much longer."

"I hope not."

"This is now the seventh day, and I can remain only three days more. Then I must return to London."

"Oh!"

"I wish to ask you to be in readiness, as I may call on you at any hour on Tuesday or Wednesday night."

"For an expedition of the same kind as we had to-night?"

"Yes, monsieur, the very same."

"With what result?"

"The capture of Arsène Lupin," replied Sholmes.

"Do you think so?"

"I swear it, on my honour, monsieur."

Sholmes bade Ganimard goodbye and went to the nearest hotel for a few hours' sleep; after which, refreshed and with renewed confidence in himself, he returned to the rue Chalgrin, slipped two louis into the hand of the concierge, assured himself that the brothers Leroux had gone out, learned that the house belonged to a Monsieur Harmingeat, and, provided with a candle, descended to the cellar through the low door near which he had found the garnet. At the bottom of the stairs he found another exactly like it.

"I am not mistaken," he thought; "this is the means of communication. Let me see if my skeleton-key will open the cellar reserved for the tenant of the ground floor. Yes; it will. Now, I will examine those cases of wine... oh! Oh! Here are some places where the dust has been cleared away... and some footprints on the ground..."

A slight noise caused him to listen attentively. Quickly he pushed the door shut, blew out his candle and hid behind a pile of empty wine cases. After a few seconds he noticed that a portion of the wall swung on a pivot, the light of a lantern was thrown into the cellar, an arm appeared, then a man entered.

He was bent over, as if he were searching for something. He felt in the dust with his fingers and several times he threw something into a cardboard box that he carried in his left hand. Afterward he obliterated the traces of his footsteps, as well as the footprints left by Lupin and the blonde lady, and he was about to leave the cellar by the same way as he had entered, when he uttered a harsh cry and fell to the ground. Sholmes had leaped upon him. It was the work of a moment, and in the simplest manner in the world the man found himself stretched on the ground, bound and handcuffed. The Englishman leaned over him and said:

"Have you anything to say?... To tell what you know?"

The man replied by such an ironical smile that Sholmes realized the futility of questioning him. So he contented himself by exploring the pockets of his captive, but he found only a bunch of keys, a handkerchief and the small cardboard box which contained a dozen garnets similar to those which Sholmes had found.

Then what was he to do with the man? Wait until his friends came to his help and deliver all of them to the police? What good would that do? What advantage would that give him over Lupin?

He hesitated; but an examination of the box decided the question. The box bore this name and address: "Leonard, jeweler, rue de la Paix."

He resolved to abandon the man to his fate. He locked the cellar and left the house. At a branch post office he sent a telegram to Monsieur Destange, saying that he could not come that day. Then he went to see the jeweller and, handing him the garnets, said:

"Madame sent me with these stones. She wishes to have them reset."

Sholmes had struck the right key. The jeweller replied:

"Certainly; the lady telephoned to me. She said she would be here today."

Sholmes established himself on the sidewalk to wait for the lady, but it was five o'clock when he saw a heavily-veiled lady approach and enter the store. Through the window he saw her place on the counter a piece of antique jewellery set with garnets.

She went away almost immediately, walking quickly and passed through streets that were unknown to the Englishman. As it was now almost dark, he walked close behind her and followed her into a five-story house of double flats and, therefore, occupied by numerous tenants. At the second floor she stopped and entered. Two minutes later the Englishman commenced to try the keys on the bunch he had taken from the man in the rue Chalgrin. The fourth key fitted the lock.

Notwithstanding the darkness of the rooms, he perceived that they were absolutely empty, as if unoccupied, and the various doors were standing open so that he could see all the apartments. At the end of a corridor he perceived a ray of light and, by approaching on tiptoe and looking through the glass door, he saw the veiled lady who had removed her hat and dress and was now wearing a velvet dressing-gown. The discarded garments were lying on the only chair in the room and a lighted lamp stood on the mantel.

Then he saw her approach the fireplace and press what appeared to be the button of an electric bell. Immediately the panel to the right of the fireplace moved and slowly glided behind the adjoining panel, thus disclosing an opening large enough for a person to pass through. The lady disappeared through this opening, taking the lamp with her.

The operation was a very simple one. Sholmes adopted it and followed the lady. He found himself in total darkness and immediately he felt his face brushed by some soft articles. He lighted a match and found that he was in a very small room completely filled with cloaks and dresses suspended on hangers. He picked his way through until he reached a door that was draped with a portiere. He peeped through and, behold, the blonde lady was there, under his eyes, and almost within reach of his hand.

She extinguished the lamp and turned on the electric lights. Then for the first time Herlock Sholmes obtained a good look at her face. He was amazed. The woman, whom he had overtaken after so much trouble and after so many tricks and manoeuvres, was none other than Clotilde Destange.

Clotilde Destange, the assassin of the Baron d'Hautrec and the thief who stole the blue diamond! Clotilde Destange, the mysterious friend of Arsène Lupin! And the blonde lady!

"Yes, I am only a stupid ass," thought Herlock Sholmes at that moment. "Because Lupin's friend was a blonde and Clotilde is a brunette, I never dreamed that they were the same person. But how could the blonde lady remain a blonde after the murder of the baron and the theft of the diamond?"

Sholmes could see a portion of the room; it was a boudoir, furnished with the most delightful luxury and exquisite taste, and adorned with beautiful tapestries and costly ornaments. A mahogany couch, upholstered in silk, was located on the side of the room opposite the door at which Sholmes was standing. Clotilde was sitting on this couch, motionless, her face covered by her hands. Then he perceived that she was weeping. Great tears rolled down her pale cheeks and fell, drop by drop, on the velvet corsage. The tears came thick and fast, as if their source were inexhaustible.

A door silently opened behind her and Arsène Lupin entered. He looked at her for a long time without making his presence known; then he approached her, knelt at her feet, pressed her head to his breast, folded her in his arms, and his actions indicated an infinite measure of love and sympathy. For a time not a word was uttered, but her tears became less abundant.

"I was so anxious to make you happy," he murmured.

"I am happy."

"No; you are crying... Your tears break my heart, Clotilde."

The caressing and sympathetic tone of his voice soothed her, and she listened to him with an eager desire for hope and happiness. Her features were softened by a smile, and yet how sad a smile! He continued to speak in a tone of tender entreaty:

"You should not be unhappy, Clotilde; you have no cause to be."

She displayed her delicate white hands and said, solemnly:

"Yes, Maxime; so long as I see those hands I shall be sad."

"Why?"

"They are stained with blood."

"Hush! Do not think of that!" exclaimed Lupin. "The dead is past and gone. Do not resurrect it."

And he kissed the long, delicate hand, while she regarded him with a brighter smile as if each kiss effaced a portion of that dreadful memory.

"You must love me, Maxime; you must—because no woman will ever love you as I do. For your sake, I have done many things, not at your order or request, but in obedience to your secret desires. I have done things at which my will and conscience revolted, but there was some unknown power that I could not resist. What I did I did involuntarily, mechanically, because it helped you, because you wished it... and I am ready to do it again tomorrow... and always."

"Ah, Clotilde," he said, bitterly, "why did I draw you into my adventurous life? I should have remained the Maxime Bermond that you loved five years ago, and not have let you know the... other man that I am."

She replied in a low voice:

"I love the other man, also, and I have nothing to regret."

"Yes, you regret your past life—the free and happy life you once enjoyed."

"I have no regrets when you are here," she said, passionately. "All faults and crimes disappear when I see you. When you are away I may suffer, and weep, and be horrified at what I have done; but when you come it is all forgotten. Your love wipes it all away. And I am happy again... But you must love me!"

"I do not love you on compulsion, Clotilde. I love you simply because... I love you."

"Are you sure of it?"

"I am just as sure of my own love as I am of yours. Only my life is a very active and exciting one, and I cannot spend as much time with you as I would like—just now."

"What is it? Some new danger? Tell me!"

"Oh! Nothing serious. Only..."

"Only what?" she asked.

"Well, he is on our track."

"Who? Herlock Sholmes?"

"Yes; it was he who dragged Ganimard into that affair at the Hungarian restaurant. It was he who instructed the two policemen to watch the house in the rue Chalgrin. I have proof of it. Ganimard searched the house this morning and Sholmes was with him. Besides—"

"Besides? What?"

"Well, there is another thing. One of our men is missing."

"Who?"

"Jeanniot."

"The concierge?"

"Yes."

"Why, I sent him to the rue Chalgrin this morning to pick up the garnets that fell out of my brooch."

"There is no doubt, then, that Sholmes caught him."

"No; the garnets were delivered to the jeweller in the rue de la Paix."

"Then, what has become of him!"

"Oh! Maxime, I am afraid."

"There is nothing to be afraid of, but I confess the situation is very serious. What does he know? Where does he hide himself? His isolation is his strong card. I cannot reach him."

"What are you going to do?"

"Act with extreme prudence, Clotilde. Some time ago I decided to change my residence to a safer place, and Sholmes' appearance on the scene has prompted me to do so at once. When a man like that is on your track, you must be prepared for the worst. Well, I am making my preparations. Day after tomorrow, Wednesday, I shall move. At noon it will be finished. At two o'clock I shall leave the place, after removing the last trace of our residence there, which will be no small matter. Until then—"

"Well?"

"Until then we must not see each other and no one must see you, Clotilde. Do not go out. I have no fear for myself, but I have for you."

"That Englishman cannot possibly reach me."

"I am not so sure of that. He is a dangerous man. Yesterday I came here to search the cupboard that contains all of Monsieur Destange's old papers and records. There is danger there. There is danger everywhere. I feel that he is watching us—that he is drawing his net around us closer and closer. It is one of those intuitions which never deceive me."

"In that case, Maxime, go, and think no more of my tears. I shall be brave, and wait patiently until the danger is past. Adieu, Maxime."

They held one another for some time in a last fond embrace. And it was she that gently pushed him outside. Sholmes could hear the sound of their voices in the distance.

Emboldened by the necessities of the situation and the urgent need of bringing his investigation to a speedy termination, Sholmes proceeded to make an examination of the house in which he now found himself. He passed through Clotilde's boudoir into a corridor, at the end of which there was a stairway leading to the lower floor; he was about to descend this stairway when he heard voices below, which caused him to change his route. He followed the corridor, which was a circular one, and discovered another stairway, which he descended and found himself amidst surroundings that bore a familiar appearance. He passed through a door that stood partly open and entered a large circular room. It was Monsieur Destange's library.

"Ah! splendid!" he exclaimed. "Now I understand everything. The boudoir of Mademoiselle Clotilde—the blonde Lady—communicates with a room in the adjoining house, and that house does not front on the Place Malesherbes, but upon an adjacent street, the rue Montchanin, if I remember the name correctly... And I now understand how Clotilde Destange can meet her lover and at the same time create the impression that she never leaves the house; and I understand also how Arsène Lupin was enabled to make his mysterious entrance to the gallery last night. Ah! There must be another connection between the library and the adjoining room. One more house full of ways that are dark! And no doubt Lucien Destange was the architect, as usual!... I should take advantage of this opportunity to examine the contents of the cupboard and perhaps learn the location of other houses with secret passages constructed by Monsieur Destange."

Sholmes ascended to the gallery and concealed himself behind some draperies, where he remained until late in the evening. At last a servant came and turned off the electric lights. An hour later the Englishman, by the light of his lantern, made his way to the cupboard. As he had surmised, it contained the architect's old papers, plans, specifications and books of account. It also contained a series of registers, arranged according to date, and Sholmes, having selected those of the most recent dates, searched in the indexes for the name "Harmingeat." He found it in one of the registers with a reference to page 63. Turning to that page, he read:

"Harmingeat, 40 rue Chalgrin."

This was followed by a detailed account of the work done in and about the installation of a furnace in the house. And in the margin of the book someone had written these words: "See account M.B."

"Ah! I thought so!" said Sholmes; "the account M.B. is the one I want. I shall learn from it the actual residence of Monsieur Lupin."

It was morning before he found that important account. It comprised sixteen pages, one of which was a copy of the page on which was described the work done for Mon. Harmingeat of the rue Chalgrin. Another page described the work performed for Mon. Vatinel as owner of the house at No. 25 rue Clapeyron.

Another page was reserved for the Baron d'Hautrec, 134 avenue Henri-Martin; another was devoted to the Château de Crozon, and the eleven other pages to various owners of houses in Paris.

Sholmes made a list of those eleven names and addresses; after which he returned the books to their proper places, opened a window, jumped out onto the deserted street and closed the shutters behind him.

When he reached his room at the hotel he lighted his pipe with all the solemnity with which he was wont to characterize that act, and amidst clouds of smoke he studied the deductions that might be drawn from the account of M.B., or rather, from the account of Maxime Bermond alias Arsène Lupin.

At eight o'clock he sent the following message to Ganimard:

> "I expect to pass through the rue Pergolese this forenoon and will inform you of a person whose arrest is of the highest importance. In any event, be at home tonight and tomorrow until noon and have at least thirty men at your service."

Then he engaged an automobile at the stand on the boulevard, choosing one whose chauffeur looked good-natured but dull-witted, and instructed him to drive to the Place Malesherbes, where he stopped him about one hundred feet from Monsieur Destange's house.

"My boy, close your carriage," he said to the chauffeur; "turn up the collar of your coat, for the wind is cold, and wait patiently. At the end of an hour and a half, crank up your machine. When I return we will go to the rue Pergolese."

As he was ascending the steps leading to the door a doubt entered his mind. Was it not a mistake on his part to be spending his time on the affairs of the blonde Lady, while Arsène Lupin was preparing to move? Would he not be better engaged in trying to find the abode of his adversary amongst the eleven houses on his list?

"Ah!" he exclaimed, "when the blonde Lady becomes my prisoner, I shall be master of the situation."

And he rang the bell.

Monsieur Destange was already in the library. They had been working only a few minutes, when Clotilde entered, bade her father good morning, entered the adjoining parlour and sat down to write. From his place Sholmes could see her leaning over the table and from time to time absorbed in deep meditation. After a short time he picked up a book and said to Monsieur Destange:

"Here is a book that Mademoiselle Destange asked me to bring to her when I found it."

He went into the little parlour, stood before Clotilde in such a manner that her father could not see her, and said:

"I am Monsieur Stickmann, your father's new secretary."

"Ah!" said Clotilde, without moving, "my father has changed his secretary? I didn't know it."

"Yes, mademoiselle, and I desire to speak with you."

"Kindly take a seat, monsieur; I have finished."

She added a few words to her letter, signed it, enclosed it in the envelope, sealed it, pushed her writing material away, rang the telephone, got in communication with her dressmaker, asked the latter to hasten the completion of a travelling dress, as she required it at once, and then, turning to Sholmes, she said:

"I am at your service, monsieur. But do you wish to speak before my father? Would not that be better?"

"No, mademoiselle; and I beg of you, do not raise your voice. It is better that Monsieur Destange should not hear us."

"For whose sake is it better?"

"Yours, mademoiselle."

"I cannot agree to hold any conversation with you that my father may not hear."

"But you must agree to this. It is imperative."

Both of them arose, eye to eye. She said:

"Speak, monsieur."

Still standing, he commenced:

"You will be so good as to pardon me if I am mistaken on certain points of secondary importance. I will guarantee, however, the general accuracy of my statements."

"Can we not dispense with these preliminaries, monsieur? Or are they necessary?"

Sholmes felt the young woman was on her guard, so he replied:

"Very well; I will come to the point. Five years ago your father made the acquaintance of a certain young man called Maxime Bermond, who was introduced as a contractor or an architect, I am not sure which it was; but it was one or the other. Monsieur Destange took a liking to the young man, and as the state of his health compelled him to retire from active business, he entrusted to Monsieur Bermond the execution of certain orders he had received from some of his old customers and which seemed to come within the scope of Monsieur Bermond's ability."

Herlock Sholmes stopped. It seemed to him that the girl's pallor had increased. Yet there was not the slightest tremor in her voice when she said:

"I know nothing about the circumstances to which you refer, monsieur, and I do not see in what way they can interest me."

"In this way, mademoiselle: You know, as well as I, that Maxime Bermond is also known by the name of Arsène Lupin."

She laughed, and said:

"Nonsense! Arsène Lupin? Maxime Bermond is Arsène Lupin? Oh! No! It isn't possible!"

"I have the honour to inform you of that fact, and since you refuse to understand my meaning, I will add that Arsène Lupin has found in this house a friend—more than a friend—and accomplice, blindly and passionately devoted to him."

Without emotion, or at least with so little emotion that Sholmes was astonished at her self-control, she declared:

"I do not understand your object, monsieur, and I do not care to; but I command you to say no more and leave this house."

"I have no intention of forcing my presence on you," replied Sholmes, with equal sang-froid, "but I shall not leave this house alone."

"And who will accompany you, monsieur?"

"You will."

"I?"

"Yes, mademoiselle, we will leave this house together, and you will follow me without one word of protest."

The strange feature of the foregoing interview was the absolute coolness of the two adversaries. It bore no resemblance to an implacable duel between two powerful wills; but, judging solely from their attitude and the tone of their voices, an onlooker would have supposed their conversation to be nothing more serious than a courteous argument over some impersonal subject.

Clotilde resumed her seat without deigning to reply to the last remark of Herlock Sholmes, except by a shrug of her shoulders. Sholmes looked at his watch and said:

"It is half-past ten. We will leave here in five minutes."

"Perhaps."

"If not, I shall go to Monsieur Destange, and tell him—"

"What?"

"The truth. I will tell him of the vicious life of Maxime Bermond, and I will tell him of the double life of his accomplice."

"Of his accomplice?"

"Yes, of the woman known as the blonde Lady, of the woman who was blonde."

"What proofs will you give him?"

"I will take him to the rue Chalgrin, and show him the secret passage made by Arsène Lupin's workmen—while doing the work of which he had the control—between the houses numbered 40 and 42; the passage which you and he used two nights ago."

"Well?"

"I will then take Monsieur Destange to the house of Monsieur Detinan; we will descend the servant's stairway which was used by you and Arsène Lupin when you escaped from Ganimard, and we will search together the means of communication with the adjoining house, which fronts on the Boulevard des Batignolles, and not upon the rue Clapeyron."

"Well?"

"I will take Monsieur Destange to the château de Crozon, and it will be easy for him, who knows the nature of the work performed by Arsène Lupin in the restoration of the Château, to discover the secret passages constructed there by his workmen. It will thus be established that those passages allowed the blonde Lady to make a nocturnal visit to the Countess' room and take the blue diamond from the mantel; and, two weeks later, by similar means, to enter the room of Herr Bleichen and conceal the blue diamond in his tooth-powder—a strange action, I confess; a woman's revenge, perhaps; but I don't know, and I don't care."

"Well?"

"After that," said Herlock Sholmes, in a more serious tone, "I will take Monsieur Destange to 134 avenue Henri-Martin, and we will learn how the Baron d'Hautrec—"

"No, no, keep quiet," stammered the girl, struck with a sudden terror, "I forbid you!... you dare to say that it was I... you accuse me?..."

"I accuse you of having killed the Baron d'Hautrec."

"No, no, it is a lie."

"You killed the Baron d'Hautrec, mademoiselle. You entered his service under the name of Antoinette Bréhat, for the purpose of stealing the blue diamond and you killed him."

"Keep quiet, monsieur," she implored him. "Since you know so much, you must know that I did not murder the baron."

"I did not say that you murdered him, mademoiselle. Baron d'Hautrec was subject to fits of insanity that only Sister Auguste could control. She told me so herself. In her absence, he must have attacked you, and in the course of the struggle you struck him in order to save your own life. Frightened at your awful situation, you rang the bell, and fled without even taking the blue diamond from the finger of your victim. A few minutes later you returned with one of Arsène Lupin's accomplices, who was a servant in the adjoining house, you placed the baron on the bed, you put the room in order, but you were afraid to take the blue diamond. Now, I have told you what happened on that night. I repeat, you did not murder the baron, and yet it was your hand that struck the blow."

She had crossed them over her forehead—those long delicate white hands—and kept them thus for a long time. At last, loosening her fingers, she said, in a voice rent by anguish:

"And do you intend to tell all that to my father?"

"Yes; and I will tell him that I have secured as witnesses: Mademoiselle Gerbois, who will recognize the blonde Lady; Sister Auguste, who will recognize Antoinette Bréhat; and the Countess de Crozon, who will recognize Madame de Réal. That is what I shall tell him."

"You will not dare," she said, recovering her self-possession in the face of an immediate peril.

He arose, and made a step toward the library. Clotilde stopped him:

"One moment, monsieur."

She paused, reflected a moment, and then, perfect mistress of herself, said:

"You are Herlock Sholmes?"

"Yes."

"What do you want of me?"

"What do I want? I am fighting a duel with Arsène Lupin, and I must win. The contest is now drawing to a climax, and I have an idea that a hostage as precious as you will give me an important advantage over my adversary. Therefore, you will follow me, mademoiselle; I will entrust you to one of my friends. As soon as the duel is ended, you will be set at liberty."

"Is that all?"

"That is all. I do not belong to the police service of this country, and, consequently, I do not consider that I am under any obligation... to cause your arrest."

She appeared to have come to a decision... yet she required a momentary respite. She closed her eyes, the better to concentrate her thoughts. Sholmes looked at her in surprise; she was now so tranquil and, apparently, indifferent to the dangers which threatened her. Sholmes thought: Does she believe that she is in danger? Probably not—since Lupin protects her. She has confidence in him. She believes that Lupin is omnipotent, and infallible.

"Mademoiselle," he said, "I told you that we would leave here in five minutes. That time has almost expired."

"Will you permit me to go to my room, monsieur, to get some necessary articles?"

"Certainly, mademoiselle; and I will wait for you in the rue Montchanin. Jeanniot, the concierge, is a friend of mine."

"Ah! you know..." she said, visibly alarmed.

"I know many things."

"Very well. I will ring for the maid."

The maid brought her hat and jacket. Then Sholmes said:

"You must give Monsieur Destange some reason for our departure, and, if possible, let your excuse serve for an absence of several days."

"That shall not be necessary. I shall be back very soon."

They exchanged defiant glances and an ironic smile.

"What faith you have in him!" said Sholmes.

"Absolute."

"He does everything well, doesn't he? He succeeds in everything he undertakes. And whatever he does receives your approval and cooperation."

"I love him," she said, with a touch of passion in her voice.

"And you think that he will save you?"

She shrugged her shoulders, and, approaching her father, she said:

"I am going to deprive you of Monsieur Stickmann. We are going to the National Library."

"You will return for luncheon?"

"Perhaps... no, I think not... but don't be uneasy."

Then she said to Sholmes, in a firm voice:

"I am at your service, monsieur."

"Absolutely?"

"Quite so."

"I warn you that if you attempt to escape, I shall call the police and have you arrested. Do not forget that the blonde Lady is on parole."

"I give you my word of honour that I shall not attempt to escape."

"I believe you. Now, let us go."

They left the house together, as he had predicted.

The automobile was standing where Sholmes had left it. As they approached it, Sholmes could hear the rumbling of the motor. He opened the door, asked Clotilde to enter, and took a seat beside her. The machine started at once, gained the exterior boulevards, the avenue Hoche and the avenue de la Grande-Armée. Sholmes was considering his plans. He thought:

"Ganimard is at home. I will leave the girl in his care. Shall I tell him who she is? No, he would take her to prison at once, and that would spoil everything. When I am alone, I can consult my list of addresses taken from the 'account M.B.,' and run them down. Tonight, or tomorrow morning at the latest, I shall go to Ganimard, as I agreed, and deliver into his hands Arsène Lupin and all his band."

He rubbed his hand, gleefully, at the thought that his duel with Lupin was drawing to a close, and he could not see any serious obstacle in the way of his success. And, yielding to an irrepressible desire to give vent to his feelings—an unusual desire on his part—he exclaimed:

"Excuse me, mademoiselle, if I am unable to conceal my satisfaction and delight. The battle has been a difficult one, and my success is, therefore, more enjoyable."

"A legitimate success, monsieur, of which you have a just right to be proud."

"Thank you. But where are we going? The chauffeur must have misunderstood my directions."

At that moment they were leaving Paris by the gate de Neuilly. That was strange, as the rue Pergolese is not outside the fortifications. Sholmes lowered the glass, and said:

"Chauffeur, you have made a mistake... Rue Pergolese!"

The man made no reply. Sholmes repeated, in a louder voice:

"I told you to go to the rue Pergolese."

Still the man did not reply.

"Ah! but you are deaf, my friend. Or is he doing it on purpose? We are very much out of our way... Rue Pergolese!... Turn back at once!... Rue Pergolese!"

The chauffeur made no sign of having heard the order. The Englishman fretted with impatience. He looked at Clotilde; a mysterious smile played upon her lips.

"Why do you laugh?" he said. "It is an awkward mistake, but it won't help you."

"Of course not," she replied.

Then an idea occurred to him. He rose and made a careful scrutiny of the chauffeur. His shoulders were not so broad; his bearing was not so stiff and mechanical. A cold perspiration covered his forehead and his hands clenched with sudden fear, as his mind was seized with the conviction that the chauffeur was Arsène Lupin.

"Well, Monsieur Sholmes, what do you think of our little ride?"

"Delightful, monsieur, really delightful," replied Sholmes.

Never in his life had he experienced so much difficulty in uttering a few simple words without a tremor, or without betraying his feelings in his voice. But quickly, by a sort of reaction, a flood of hatred and rage burst its bounds, overcame his self-control, and, brusquely drawing his revolver, he pointed it at Mademoiselle Destange.

"Lupin, stop, this minute, this second, or I fire at mademoiselle."

"I advise you to aim at the cheek if you wish to hit the temple," replied Lupin, without turning his head.

"Maxime, don't go so fast," said Clotilde, "the pavement is slippery and I am very timid."

She was smiling; her eyes were fixed on the pavement, over which the carriage was traveling at enormous speed.

"Let him stop! Let him stop!" said Sholmes to her, wild with rage, "I warn you that I am desperate."

The barrel of the revolver brushed the waving locks of her hair. She replied, calmly:

"Maxime is so imprudent. He is going so fast, I am really afraid of some accident."

Sholmes returned the weapon to his pocket and seized the handle of the door, as if to alight, despite the absurdity of such an act. Clotilde said to him:

"Be careful, monsieur, there is an automobile behind us."

He leaned over. There was an automobile close behind; a large machine of formidable aspect with its sharp prow and blood-red body, and holding four men clad in fur coats.

"Ah! I am well guarded," thought Sholmes. "I may as well be patient."

He folded his arms across his chest with that proud air of submission so frequently assumed by heroes when fate has turned against them. And while they crossed the river Seine and rushed through Suresnes, Rueil and Chatou, motionless and resigned, controlling his actions and his passions, he tried to explain to his own satisfaction by what miracle Arsène Lupin had substituted himself for the chauffeur. It was quite improbable that the honest-looking fellow he had selected on the boulevard that morning was an accomplice placed there in advance. And yet Arsène Lupin had received a warning in some way, and it must have been after he, Sholmes, had approached Clotilde in the house, because no one could have suspected his project prior to that time. Since then, Sholmes had not allowed Clotilde out of his sight.

Then an idea struck him: the telephone communication desired by Clotilde and her conversation with the dressmaker. Now, it was all quite clear to him. Even before he had spoken to her, simply upon his request to speak to her as the new secretary of Monsieur Destange, she had scented the danger, surmised the name and purpose of the visitor, and, calmly, naturally, as if she were performing a commonplace action of her every-day life, she had called Arsène Lupin to her assistance by some preconcerted signal.

How Arsène Lupin had come and caused himself to be substituted for the chauffeur were matters of trifling importance. That which affected Sholmes, even to the point of appeasing his fury, was the recollection of that incident whereby an ordinary woman, a sweetheart it is true, mastering her nerves, controlling her features, and subjugating the expression of her eyes, had completely deceived the astute detective Herlock Sholmes. How difficult to overcome an adversary who is aided by such confederates, and who, by the mere force of his authority, inspires in a woman so much courage and strength!

They crossed the Seine and climbed the hill at Saint-Germain; but, some five hundred metres beyond that town, the automobile slackened its speed. The other automobile advanced, and the two stopped, side by side. There was no one else in the neighbourhood.

"Monsieur Sholmes," said Lupin, "kindly exchange to the other machine. Ours is really a very slow one."

"Indeed!" said Sholmes, calmly, convinced that he had no choice.

"Also, permit me to loan you a fur coat, as we will travel quite fast and the air is cool. And accept a couple of sandwiches, as we cannot tell when we will dine."

The four men alighted from the other automobile. One of them approached, and, as he raised his goggles, Sholmes recognized in him the gentleman in the frock coat that he had seen at the Hungarian restaurant. Lupin said to him:

"You will return this machine to the chauffeur from whom I hired it. He is waiting in the first wine-shop to the right as you go up the rue Legendre. You will give him the balance of the thousand francs I promised him... Ah! yes, kindly give your goggles to Monsieur Sholmes."

He talked to Mlle. Destange for a moment, then took his place at the wheel and started, with Sholmes at his side and one of his men behind him. Lupin had not exaggerated when he said "we will travel quite fast." From the beginning he set a breakneck pace. The horizon rushed to meet them, as if attracted by some mysterious force, and disappeared instantly as though swallowed up in an abyss, into which many other things, such as trees, houses, fields and forests, were hurled with the tumultuous fury and haste of a torrent as it approached the cataract.

Sholmes and Lupin did not exchange a word. Above their heads the leaves of the poplars made a great noise like the waves of the sea, rhythmically arranged by the regular spacing of the trees. And the towns swept by like spectres: Manteo, Vernon, Gaillon. From one hill to the other, from Bon-Secours to Canteleu, Rouen, its suburbs, its harbour, its miles of wharves, Rouen seemed like the straggling street of a country village. And this was Duclair, Caudebec, the country of Caux which they skimmed over in their terrific flight, and Lillebonne, and Quillebeuf. Then, suddenly, they found themselves on the banks of the Seine, at the extremity of a little wharf, beside which lay a staunch sea-going yacht that emitted great volumes of black smoke from its funnel.

The automobile stopped. In two hours they had travelled over forty leagues.

A man, wearing a blue uniform and a goldlaced cap, came forward and saluted. Lupin said to him:

"All ready, captain? Did you receive my telegram?"

"Yes, I got it."

"Is *The Swallow* ready?"

"Yes, monsieur."

"Come, Monsieur Sholmes."

The Englishman looked around, saw a group of people on the terrace in front of a café, hesitated a moment, then, realizing that before he could secure any assistance he would be seized, carried aboard and placed in the bottom of the hold, he crossed the gang-plank and followed Lupin into the captain's cabin. It was quite a large room, scrupulously clean, and presented a cheerful appearance with its varnished woodwork and polished brass. Lupin closed the door and addressed Sholmes abruptly, and almost rudely, as he said:

"Well, what do you know?"

"Everything."

"Everything? Come, be precise."

His voice contained no longer that polite, if ironical, tone, which he had affected when speaking to the Englishman. Now, his voice had the imperious tone of a master accustomed to command and accustomed to be obeyed—even by a Herlock Sholmes. They measured each other by their looks, enemies now—open and implacable foes. Lupin spoke again, but in a milder tone:

"I have grown weary of your pursuit, and do not intend to waste any more time in avoiding the traps you lay for me. I warn you that my treatment of you will depend on your reply. Now, what do you know?"

"Everything, monsieur."

Arsène Lupin controlled his temper and said, in a jerky manner:

"I will tell you what you know. You know that, under the name of Maxime Bermond, I have ... *improved* fifteen houses that were originally constructed by Monsieur Destange."

"Yes."

"Of those fifteen houses, you have seen four."

"Yes."

"And you have a list of the other eleven."

"Yes."

"You made that list at Monsieur Destange's house on that night, no doubt."

"Yes."

"And you have an idea that, amongst those eleven houses, there is one that I have kept for the use of myself and my friends, and you have intrusted to Ganimard the task of finding my retreat."

"No."

"What does that signify?"

"It signifies that I choose to act alone, and do not want his help."

"Then I have nothing to fear, since you are in my hands."

"You have nothing to fear as long as I remain in your hands."

"You mean that you will not remain?"

"Yes."

Arsène Lupin approached the Englishman and, placing his hand on the latter's shoulder, said:

"Listen, monsieur; I am not in a humour to argue with you, and, unfortunately for you, you are not in a position to choose. So let us finish our business."

"Very well."

"You are going to give me your word of honour that you will not try to escape from this boat until you arrive in English waters."

"I give you my word of honour that I shall escape if I have an opportunity," replied the indomitable Sholmes.

"But, sapristi! you know quite well that at a word from me you would soon be rendered helpless. All these men will obey me blindly. At a sign from me they would place you in irons—"

"Irons can be broken."

"And throw you overboard ten miles from shore."

"I can swim."

"I hadn't thought of that," said Lupin, with a laugh. "Excuse me, master... and let us finish. You will agree that I must take the measures necessary to protect myself and my friends."

"Certainly; but they will be useless."

"And yet you do not wish me to take them."

"It is your duty."

"Very well, then."

Lupin opened the door and called the captain and two sailors. The latter seized the Englishman, bound him hand and foot, and tied him to the captain's bunk.

"That will do," said Lupin. "It was only on account of your obstinacy and the unusual gravity of the situation, that I ventured to offer you this indignity."

The sailors retired. Lupin said to the captain:

"Let one of the crew remain here to look after Monsieur Sholmes, and you can give him as much of your own company as possible. Treat him with all due respect and consideration. He is not a prisoner, but a guest. What time have you, captain?"

"Five minutes after two."

Lupin consulted his watch, then looked at the clock that was attached to the wall of the cabin.

"Five minutes past two is right. How long will it take you to reach Southampton?"

"Nine hours, easy going."

"Make it eleven. You must not land there until after the departure of the midnight boat, which reaches Havre at eight o'clock in the morning. Do you understand, captain? Let me repeat: As it would be very dangerous for all of us to permit Monsieur to return to France by that boat, you must not reach Southampton before one o'clock in the morning."

"I understand."

"Au revoir, master; next year, in this world or in the next."

"Until tomorrow," replied Sholmes.

A few minutes later Sholmes heard the automobile going away, and at the same time the steam puffed violently in the depths of *The Swallow*. The boat had started for England. About three o'clock the vessel left the mouth of the river and plunged into the open sea. At that moment Sholmes was lying on the captain's bunk, sound asleep.

Next morning—it being the tenth and last day of the duel between Sholmes and Lupin—the *Echo de France* published this interesting bit of news:

"Yesterday a judgment of ejectment was entered in the case of Arsène Lupin against Herlock Sholmes, the English detective. Although signed at noon, the judgment was executed the same day. At one o'clock this morning Sholmes was landed at Southampton."

Chapter 6

SECOND ARREST OF ARSÈNE LUPIN

Since eight o'clock a dozen moving-vans had encumbered the rue Crevaux between the avenue du Bois-de-Boulogne and the avenue Bugeaud. Mon. Felix Davey was leaving the apartment in which he lived on the fourth floor of No. 8; and Mon. Dubreuil, who had united into a single apartment the fifth floor of the same house and the fifth floor of the two adjoining houses, was moving on the same day—a mere coincidence, since the gentlemen were unknown to each other—the vast collection of furniture regarding which so many foreign agents visited him every day.

A circumstance which had been noticed by some of the neighbours, but was not spoken of until later, was this: None of the twelve vans bore the name and address of the owner, and none of the men accompanying them visited the neighbouring wine shops. They worked so diligently that the furniture was all out by eleven o'clock. Nothing remained but those scraps of papers and rags that are always left behind in the corners of the empty rooms.

Mon. Felix Davey, an elegant young man, dressed in the latest fashion, carried in his hand a walking-stick, the weight of which indicated that its owner possessed extraordinary biceps—Mon. Felix Davey walked calmly away and took a seat on a bench in the avenue du Bois-de-Boulogne facing the rue Pergolese. Close to him a woman, dressed in a neat but inexpensive costume, was reading a newspaper, whilst a child was playing with a shovel in a heap of sand.

After a few minutes Felix Davey spoke to the woman, without turning his head:

"Ganimard!"

"Went out at nine o'clock this morning."

"Where?"

"To police headquarters."

"Alone?"

"Yes."

"No telegram during the night?"

"No."

"Do they suspect you in the house?"

"No; I do some little things for Madame Ganimard, and she tells me everything her husband does. I have been with her all morning."

"Very well. Until further orders come here every day at eleven o'clock."

He rose and walked away in the direction of the Dauphine gate, stopping at the Chinese pavilion, where he partook of a frugal repast consisting of two eggs, with some fruit and vegetables. Then he returned to the rue Crevaux and said to the concierge:

"I will just glance through the rooms and then give you the keys."

He finished his inspection of the room that he had used as a library; then he seized the end of a gas-pipe, which hung down the side of the chimney. The pipe was bent and a hole made in the elbow. To this hole he fitted a small instrument in the form of an ear-trumpet and blew into it. A slight whistling sound came by way of reply. Placing the trumpet to his mouth, he said:

"Anyone around, Dubreuil?"

"No."

"May I come up!"

"Yes."

He returned the pipe to its place, saying to himself:

"How progressive we are! Our century abounds with little inventions which render life really charming and picturesque. And so amusing!... especially when a person knows how to enjoy life as I do."

He turned one of the marble mouldings of the mantel, and the entire half of the mantel moved, and the mirror above it glided in invisible grooves, disclosing an opening and the lower steps of a stairs built in the very body of the chimney; all very clean and complete—the stairs were constructed of polished metal and the walls of white tiles. He ascended the steps, and at the fifth floor there was the same opening in the chimney. Mon. Dubreuil was waiting for him.

"Have you finished in your rooms?"

"Yes."

"Everything cleared out?"

"Yes."

"And the people?"

"Only the three men on guard."

"Very well; come on."

They ascended to the upper floor by the same means, one after the other, and there found three men, one of whom was looking through the window.

"Anything new?"

"Nothing, governor."

"All quiet in the street?"

"Yes."

"In ten minutes I will be ready to leave. You will go also. But in the meantime if you see the least suspicious movement in the street, warn me."

"I have my finger on the alarm-bell all the time."

"Dubreuil, did you tell the moving men not to touch the wire of that bell?"

"Certainly; it is working all right."

"That is all I want to know."

The two gentlemen then descended to the apartment of Felix Davey and the latter, after adjusting the marble mantel, exclaimed, joyfully:

"Dubreuil, I should like to see the man who is able to discover all the ingenious devices, warning bells, networks of electric wires and acoustic tubes, invisible passages, moving floors and hidden stairways. A real fairy-land!"

"What fame for Arsène Lupin!"

"Fame I could well dispense with. It's a pity to be compelled to leave a place so well equipped, and commence all over again, Dubreuil... and on a new model, of course, for it would never do to duplicate this. Curse Herlock Sholmes!"

"Has he returned to Paris?"

"How could he? There has been only one boat come from Southampton and it left there at midnight; only one train from Havre, leaving there at eight o'clock this morning and due in Paris at eleven fifteen. As he could not catch the midnight boat at Southampton—and the instructions to the captain on that point were explicit—he cannot reach France until this evening via Newhaven and Dieppe."

"Do you think he will come back?"

"Yes; he never gives up. He will return to Paris; but it will be too late. We will be far away."

"And Mademoiselle Destange?"

"I am to see her in an hour."

"At her house?"

"Oh! No; she will not return there for several days. But you, Dubreuil, you must hurry. The loading of our goods will take a long time and you should be there to look after them."

"Are you sure that we are not being watched?"

"By whom? I am not afraid of anyone but Sholmes."

Dubreuil retired. Felix Davey made a last tour of the apartment, picked up two or three torn letters, then, noticing a piece of chalk, he took it and, on the dark paper of the drawing-room, drew a large frame and wrote within it the following:

"*Arsène Lupin, gentleman-burglar, lived here for five years at the beginning of the twentieth century.*"

This little pleasantry seemed to please him very much. He looked at it for a moment, whistling a lively air, then said to himself:

"Now that I have placed myself in touch with the historians of future generations, I can go. You must hurry, Herlock Sholmes, as I shall leave my present abode in three minutes, and your defeat will be an accomplished fact... Two minutes more! You are keeping me waiting, Monsieur Sholmes... One minute more! Are you not coming? Well, then, I proclaim your downfall and my apotheosis. And now I make my escape. Farewell, kingdom of Arsène Lupin! I shall never see you again. Farewell to the fifty-five rooms of the six apartments over which I reigned! Farewell, my own royal bed chamber!"

His outburst of joy was interrupted by the sharp ringing of a bell, which stopped twice, started again and then ceased. It was the alarm bell.

What was wrong? What unforeseen danger? Ganimard? No; that wasn't possible!

He was on the point of returning to his library and making his escape. But, first, he went to the window. There was no one in the street. Was the enemy already in the house? He listened and thought he could discern certain confused sounds. He hesitated no longer. He ran to his library, and as he crossed the threshold he heard the noise of a key being inserted in the lock of the vestibule door.

"The deuce!" he murmured; "I have no time to lose. The house may be surrounded. The servants' stairway—impossible! Fortunately, there is the chimney."

He pushed the moulding; it did not move. He made a greater effort—still it refused to move. At the same time he had the impression that the door below opened and that he could hear footsteps.

"Good God!" he cried; "I am lost if this cursed mechanism—"

He pushed with all his strength. Nothing moved—nothing! By some incredible accident, by some evil stroke of fortune, the mechanism, which had worked only a few moments ago, would not work now.

He was furious. The block of marble remained immovable. He uttered frightful imprecations on the senseless stone. Was his escape to be prevented by that stupid obstacle? He struck the marble wildly, madly; he hammered it, he cursed it.

"Ah! What's the matter, Monsieur Lupin? You seem to be displeased about something."

Lupin turned around. Herlock Sholmes stood before him!

Herlock Sholmes!... Lupin gazed at him with squinting eyes as if his sight were defective and misleading. Herlock Sholmes in Paris! Herlock Sholmes, whom he had shipped to England only the day before as a dangerous person, now stood before him free and victorious!... Ah! Such a thing was nothing less than a miracle; it was contrary to all natural laws; it was the culmination of all that is illogical and abnormal... Herlock Sholmes here—before his face!

And when the Englishman spoke his words were tinged with that keen sarcasm and mocking politeness with which his adversary had so often lashed him. He said:

"Monsieur Lupin, in, the first place I have the honour to inform you that at this time and place I blot from my memory forever all thoughts of the miserable night that you forced me to endure in the house of Baron d'Hautrec, of the injury done to my friend Wilson, of my abduction in the automobile, and of the voyage I took yesterday under your orders, bound to a very uncomfortable couch. But the joy of this moment effaces all those bitter memories. I forgive everything. I forget everything—I wipe out the debt. I am paid—and royally paid."

Lupin made no reply. So the Englishman continued:

"Don't you think so yourself?"

He appeared to insist as if demanding an acquiescence, as a sort of receipt in regard to the part.

After a moment's reflection, during which the Englishman felt that he was scrutinized to the very depth of his soul, Lupin declared:

"I presume, monsieur, that your conduct is based upon serious motives?"

"Very serious."

"The fact that you have escaped from my captain and his crew is only a secondary incident of our struggle. But the fact that you are here before me alone—understand, alone—face to face with Arsène Lupin, leads me to think that your revenge is as complete as possible."

"As complete as possible."

"This house?"

"Surrounded."

"The two adjoining houses?"

"Surrounded."

"The apartment above this?"

"The *three* apartments on the fifth floor that were formerly occupied by Monsieur Dubreuil are surrounded."

"So that—"

"So that you are captured, Monsieur Lupin—absolutely captured."

The feelings that Sholmes had experienced during his trip in the automobile were now suffered by Lupin, the same concentrated fury, the same revolt, and also, let us admit, the same loyalty of submission to force of circumstances. Equally brave in victory or defeat.

"Our accounts are squared, monsieur," said Lupin, frankly.

The Englishman was pleased with that confession. After a short silence Lupin, now quite self-possessed, said smiling:

"And I am not sorry! It becomes monotonous to win all the time. Yesterday I had only to stretch out my hand to finish you forever. Today I belong to you. The game is yours." Lupin laughed heartily and then continued: "At last the gallery will be entertained! Lupin in prison! How will he get out? In prison!... What an adventure!... Ah! Sholmes, life is just one damn thing after another!"

He pressed his closed hands to his temples as if to suppress the tumultuous joy that surged within him, and his actions indicated that he was moved by an uncontrollable mirth. At last, when he had recovered his self-possession, he approached the detective and said:

"And now what are you waiting for?"

"What am I waiting for?"

"Yes; Ganimard is here with his men—why don't they come in?"

"I asked him not to."

"And he consented?"

"I accepted his services on condition that he would be guided by me. Besides, he thinks that Felix Davey is only an accomplice of Arsène Lupin."

"Then I will repeat my question in another form. Why did you come in alone?"

"Because I wished to speak to you alone."

"Ah! ah! you have something to say to me."

That idea seemed to please Lupin immensely. There are certain circumstances in which words are preferable to deeds.

"Monsieur Sholmes, I am sorry I cannot offer you an easy chair. How would you like that broken box? Or perhaps you would prefer the window ledge? I am sure a glass of beer would be welcome... light or dark?... But sit down, please."

"Thank you; we can talk as well standing up."

"Very well—proceed."

"I will be brief. The object of my sojourn in France was not to accomplish your arrest. If I have been led to pursue you, it was because I saw no other way to achieve my real object."

"Which was?"

"To recover the blue diamond."

"The blue diamond!"

"Certainly; since the one found in Herr Bleichen's tooth-powder was only an imitation."

"Quite right; the genuine diamond was taken by the blonde Lady. I made an exact duplicate of it and then, as I had designs on other jewels belonging to the Countess and as the Consul Herr Bleichen was already under suspicion, the aforesaid blonde Lady, in order to avert suspicion, slipped the false stone into the aforesaid Consul's luggage."

"While you kept the genuine diamond?"

"Of course."

"That diamond—I want it."

"I am very sorry, but it is impossible."

"I have promised it to the Countess de Crozon. I must have it."

"How will you get it, since it is in my possession?"

"That is precisely the reason—because it is in your possession."

"Oh! I am to give it to you?"

"Yes."

"Voluntarily?"

"I will buy it."

"Ah!" exclaimed Lupin, in an access of mirth, "you are certainly an Englishman. You treat this as a matter of business."

"It is a matter of business."

"Well? What is your offer?"

"The liberty of Mademoiselle Destange."

"Her liberty?... I didn't know she was under arrest."

"I will give Monsieur Ganimard the necessary information. When deprived of your protection, she can readily be taken."

Lupin laughed again, and said:

"My dear monsieur, you are offering me something you do not possess. Mademoiselle Destange is in a place of safety, and has nothing to fear. You must make me another offer."

The Englishman hesitated, visibly embarrassed and vexed. Then, placing his hand on the shoulder of his adversary, he said:

"And if I should propose to you—"

"My liberty?"

"No... but I can leave the room to consult with Ganimard."

"And leave me alone!"

"Yes."

"Ah! Mon dieu, what good would that be? The cursed mechanism will not work," said Lupin, at the same time savagely pushing the moulding of the mantel. He stifled a cry of surprise; this time fortune favoured him—the block of marble moved. It was his salvation; his hope of escape. In that event, why submit to the conditions imposed by Sholmes? He paced up and down the room, as if he were considering his reply. Then, in his turn, he placed his hand on the shoulder of his adversary, and said:

"All things considered, Monsieur Sholmes, I prefer to do my own business in my own way."

"But—"

"No, I don't require anyone's assistance."

"When Ganimard gets his hand on you, it will be all over. You can't escape from them."

"Who knows?"

"Come, that is foolish. Every door and window is guarded."

"Except one."

"Which?"

"*The one I will choose.*"

"Mere words! Your arrest is as good as made."

"Oh! No—not at all."

"Well?"

"I shall keep the blue diamond."

Sholmes looked at his watch, and said:

"It is now ten minutes to three. At three o'clock I shall call Ganimard."

"Well, then, we have ten minutes to chat. And to satisfy my curiosity, Monsieur Sholmes, I should like to know how you procured my address and my name of Felix Davey?"

Although his adversary's easy manner caused Sholmes some anxiety, he was willing to give Lupin the desired information since it reflected credit on his professional astuteness; so he replied:

"Your address? I got it from the blonde Lady."

"Clotilde!"

"Herself. Do you remember, yesterday morning, when I wished to take her away in the automobile, she telephoned to her dressmaker."

"Well?"

"Well, I understood, later, that you were the dressmaker. And last night, on the boat, by exercising my memory—and my memory is something I have good reason to be proud of—I was able to recollect the last two figures of your telephone number—73. Then, as I possessed a list of the houses you had 'improved,' it was an easy matter, on my arrival in Paris at eleven o'clock this morning, to search in the telephone directory and find there the name and address of Felix Davey. Having obtained that information, I asked the aid of Monsieur Ganimard."

"Admirable! I congratulate you. But bow did you manage to catch the eight o'clock train at Havre! How did you escape from *The Swallow*?"

"I did not escape."

"But—"

"You ordered the captain not to reach Southampton before one o'clock. He landed me there at midnight. I was able to catch the twelve o'clock boat for Havre."

"Did the captain betray me? I can't believe it."

"No, he did not betray you."

"Well, what then?"

"It was his watch."

"His watch?"

"Yes, I put it ahead one hour."

"How?"

"In the usual way, by turning the hands. We were sitting side by side, talking, and I was telling him some funny stories... Why! he never saw me do it."

"Bravo! A very clever trick. I shall not forget it. But the clock that was hanging on the wall of the cabin?"

"Ah! The clock was a more difficult matter, as my feet were tied, but the sailor, who guarded me during the captain's absence, was kind enough to turn the hands for me."

"He? Nonsense! He wouldn't do it."

"Oh! But he didn't know the importance of his act. I told him I must catch the first train for London, at any price, and... he allowed himself to be persuaded—"

"By means of—"

"By means of a slight gift, which the excellent fellow, loyal and true to his master, intends to send to you."

"What was it!"

"A mere trifle."

"But what?"

"The blue diamond."

"The blue diamond!"

"Yes, the false stone that you substituted for the Countess' diamond. She gave it to me."

There was a sudden explosion of violent laughter. Lupin laughed until the tears started in his eyes.

"Mon dieu, but it is funny! My false diamond palmed off on my innocent sailor! And the captain's watch! And the hands of the clock!"

Sholmes felt that the duel between him and Lupin was keener than ever. His marvellous instinct warned him that, behind his adversary's display of mirth, there was a shrewd intellect debating the ways and means to escape. Gradually Lupin approached the Englishman, who recoiled, and, unconsciously, slipped his hand into his watch-pocket.

"It is three o'clock, Monsieur Lupin."

"Three o'clock, already! What a pity! We were enjoying our chat so much."

"I am waiting for your answer."

"My answer? Mon dieu! But you are particular!... And so this is the last move in our little game—and the stake is my liberty!"

"Or the blue diamond."

"Very well. It's your play. What are you going to do!"

"I play the king," said Sholmes, as he fired his revolver.

"And I the ace," replied Lupin, as he struck at Sholmes with his fist.

Sholmes had fired into the air, as a signal to Ganimard, whose assistance he required. But Lupin's fist had caught Sholmes in the stomach, and caused him to double up with pain. Lupin rushed to the fireplace and set the marble slab in motion... Too late! The door opened.

"Surrender, Lupin, or I fire!"

Ganimard, doubtless stationed closer than Lupin had thought, Ganimard was there, with his revolver turned on Lupin. And behind Ganimard there were twenty men, strong and ruthless fellows, who would beat him like a dog at the least sign of resistance.

"Hands down! I surrender!" said Lupin, calmly; and he folded his arms across his breast.

Everyone was amazed. In the room, divested of its furniture and hangings, Arsène Lupin's words sounded like an echo... "I surrender!"... It seemed incredible. No one would have been astonished if he had suddenly vanished through a trap, or if a section of the wall had rolled away and allowed him to escape. But he surrendered!

Ganimard advanced, nervously, and with all the gravity that the importance of the occasion demanded, he placed his hand on the shoulder of his adversary, and had the infinite pleasure of saying:

"I arrest you, Arsène Lupin."

"Brrr!" said Lupin, "you make me shiver, my dear Ganimard. What a lugubrious face! One would imagine you were speaking over the grave of a friend. For Heaven's sake, don't assume such a funereal air."

"I arrest you."

"Don't let that worry you! In the name of the law, of which he is a well-deserving pillar, Ganimard, the celebrated Parisian detective, arrests the wicked Arsène Lupin. An historic event, of which you will appreciate the true importance... And it is the second time that it has happened. Bravo, Ganimard, you are sure of advancement in your chosen profession!"

And he held out his wrists for the hand-cuffs. Ganimard adjusted them in a most solemn manner. The numerous policemen, despite their customary presumption and the bitterness of their feelings toward Lupin, conducted themselves with becoming modesty, astonished at being permitted to gaze upon that mysterious and intangible creature.

"My poor Lupin," sighed our hero, "what would your aristocratic friends say if they should see you in this humiliating position?"

He pulled his wrists apart with all his strength. The veins in his forehead expanded. The links of the chain cut into his flesh. The chain fell off—broken.

"Another, comrades, that one was useless."

They placed two on him this time.

"Quite right," he said. "You cannot be too careful."

Then, counting the detectives and policemen, he said:

"How many are you, my friends? Twenty-five? Thirty? That's too many. I can't do anything. Ah! If there had been only fifteen!"

There was something fascinating about Lupin; it was the fascination of the great actor who plays his role with spirit and understanding, combined with assurance and ease. Sholmes regarded him as one might regard a beautiful painting with a due appreciation of all its perfection in colouring and technique. And he really thought that it was an equal struggle between those thirty men on one side, armed as they were with all the strength and majesty of the law, and, on the other side, that solitary individual, unarmed and handcuffed. Yes, the two sides were well-matched.

"Well, master," said Lupin to the Englishman, "this is your work. Thanks to you, Lupin is going to rot on the damp straw of a dungeon. Confess that your conscience pricks you a little, and that your soul is filled with remorse."

In spite of himself, Sholmes shrugged his shoulders, as if to say: "It's your own fault."

"Never! Never!" exclaimed Lupin. "Give you the blue diamond? Oh! No, it has cost me too much trouble. I intend to keep it. On my occasion of my first visit to you in London—which will probably be next month—I will tell you my reasons. But will you be in London next month? Or do you prefer Vienna? Or Saint Petersburg?"

Then Lupin received a surprise. A bell commenced to ring. It was not the alarm-bell, but the bell of the telephone which was located between the two windows of the room and had not yet been removed.

The telephone! Ah! Who could it be? Who was about to fall into this unfortunate trap? Arsène Lupin exhibited an excess of rage against the unlucky instrument as if he would like to break it into a thousand pieces and thus stifle the mysterious voice that was calling for him. But it was Ganimard who took down the receiver, and said:

"Hello!... Hello!... number 648.73 ... yes, this is it."

Then Sholmes stepped up, and, with an air of authority, pushed Ganimard aside, took the receiver, and covered the transmitter with his handkerchief in order to obscure the tone of his voice. At that moment he glanced toward Lupin, and the look which they exchanged indicated that the same idea had occurred to each of them, and that they foresaw the ultimate result of that theory: it was the blonde Lady who was telephoning. She wished to telephone to Felix Davey, or rather to Maxime Bermond, and it was to Sholmes she was about to speak. The Englishman said:

"Hello ... Hello!"

Then, after a silence, he said:

"Yes, it is I, Maxime."

The drama had commenced and was progressing with tragic precision. Lupin, the irrepressible and nonchalant Lupin, did not attempt to conceal his anxiety, and he strained every nerve in a desire to hear or, at least, to divine the purport of the conversation. And Sholmes continued, in reply to the mysterious voice:

"Hello!... Hello!... Yes, everything has been moved, and I am just ready to leave here and meet you as we agreed... Where?... Where you are now... Don't believe that he is here yet!..."

Sholmes stopped, seeking for words. It was clear that he was trying to question the girl without betraying himself, and that he was ignorant of her whereabouts. Moreover, Ganimard's presence seemed to embarrass him... Ah! if some miracle would only interrupt that cursed conversation! Lupin prayed for it with all his strength, with all the intensity of his incited nerves! After a momentary pause, Sholmes continued:

"Hello!... Hello!... Do you hear me?... I can't hear you very well... Can scarcely make out what you say... Are you listening?

Well, I think you had better return home... No danger now... But he is in England! I have received a telegram from Southampton announcing his arrival."

The sarcasm of those words! Sholmes uttered them with an inexpressible comfort. And he added:

"Very well, don't lose any time. I will meet you there."

He hung up the receiver.

"Monsieur Ganimard, can you furnish me with three men?"

"For the blonde Lady, eh?"

"Yes."

"You know who she is, and where she is?"

"Yes."

"Good! That settles Monsieur Lupin... Folenfant, take two men, and go with Monsieur Sholmes."

The Englishman departed, accompanied by the three men.

The game was ended. The blonde Lady was, also, about to fall into the hands of the Englishman. Thanks to his commendable persistence and to a combination of fortuitous circumstances, the battle had resulted in a victory for the detective, and in irreparable disaster for Lupin.

"Monsieur Sholmes!"

The Englishman stopped.

"Monsieur Lupin?"

Lupin was clearly shattered by this final blow. His forehead was marked by deep wrinkles. He was sullen and dejected. However, he pulled himself together, and, notwithstanding his defeat, he exclaimed, in a cheerful tone:

"You will concede that fate has been against me. A few minutes ago, it prevented my escape through that chimney, and delivered me into your hands. Now, by means of the telephone, it presents you with the blonde Lady. I submit to its decrees."

"What do you mean?"

"I mean that I am ready to re-open our negotiation."

Sholmes took Ganimard aside and asked, in a manner that did not permit a reply, the authority to exchange a few words with the prisoner. Then he approached Lupin, and said, in a sharp, nervous tone:

"What do you want?"

"Mademoiselle Destange's liberty."

"You know the price."

"Yes."

"And you accept?"

"Yes; I accept your terms."

"Ah!" said the Englishman, in surprise, "but... you refused... for yourself—"

"Yes, I can look out for myself, Monsieur Sholmes, but now the question concerns a young woman ... and a woman I love. In France, understand, we have very decided ideas about such things. And Lupin has the same feelings as other people."

He spoke with simplicity and candour. Sholmes replied by an almost imperceptible inclination of his head, and murmured:

"Very well, the blue diamond."

"Take my cane, there, at the end of the mantel. Press on the head of the cane with one hand, and, with the other, turn the iron ferrule at the bottom."

Holmes took the cane and followed the directions. As he did so, the head of the cane divided and disclosed a cavity which contained a small ball of wax which, in turn, enclosed a diamond. He examined it. It was the blue diamond.

"Monsieur Lupin, Mademoiselle Destange is free."

"Is her future safety assured? Has she nothing to fear from you?"

"Neither from me, nor anyone else."

"How can you manage it?"

"Quite easily. I have forgotten her name and address."

"Thank you. And au revoir—for I will see you again, sometime, Monsieur Sholmes?"

"I have no doubt of it."

Then followed an animated conversation between Sholmes and Ganimard, which was abruptly terminated by the Englishman, who said:

"I am very sorry, Monsieur Ganimard, that we cannot agree on that point, but I have no time to waste trying to convince you. I leave for England within an hour."

"But... the blonde Lady?"

"I do not know such a person."

"And yet, a moment ago—"

"You must take the affair as it stands. I have delivered Arsène Lupin into your hands. Here is the blue diamond, which you will have the pleasure of returning to the Countess de Crozon. What more do you want?"

"The blonde Lady."

"Find her."

Sholmes pulled his cap down over his forehead and walked rapidly away, like a man who is accustomed to go as soon as his business is finished.

"Bon voyage, monsieur," cried Lupin, "and, believe me, I shall never forget the friendly way in which our little business affairs have been arranged. My regards to Monsieur Wilson."

Not receiving any reply, Lupin added, sneeringly:

"That is what is called 'taking British leave.' Ah! their insular dignity lacks the flower of courtesy by which we are distinguished. Consider for a moment, Ganimard, what a charming exit a Frenchman would have made under similar circumstances! With what exquisite courtesy he would have masked his triumph!... But, God bless me, Ganimard, what are you doing? Making a search? Come, what's the use? There is nothing left—not even a scrap of paper. I assure you my archives are in a safe place."

"I am not so sure of that," replied Ganimard. "I must search everything."

Lupin submitted to the operation. Held by two detectives and surrounded by the others, he patiently endured the proceedings for twenty minutes, then he said:

"Hurry up, Ganimard, and finish!"

"You are in a hurry."

"Of course I am. An important appointment."

"At the police station?"

"No; in the city."

"Ah! At what time?"

"Two o'clock."

"It is three o'clock now."

"Just so; I will be late. And punctuality is one of my virtues."

"Well, give me five minutes."

"Not a second more," said Lupin.

"I am doing my best to expedite—"

"Oh! Don't talk so much... Still searching that cupboard? It is empty."

"Here are some letters."

"Old invoices, I presume!"

"No; a packet tied with a ribbon."

"A red ribbon? Oh! Ganimard, for God's sake, don't untie it!"

"From a woman?"

"Yes."

"A woman of the world?"

"The best in the world."

"Her name?"

"Madame Ganimard."

"Very funny! Very funny!" exclaimed the detective.

At that moment the men, who had been sent to search the other rooms, returned and announced their failure to find anything. Lupin laughed and said:

"Parbleu! Did you expect to find my visiting list, or evidence of my business relations with the Emperor of Germany? But I can tell you what you should investigate, Ganimard: All the little mysteries of this apartment. For instance, that gas-pipe is a speaking tube. That chimney contains a stairway. That wall is hollow. And the marvellous system of bells! Ah! Ganimard, just press that button!"

Ganimard obeyed.

"Did you hear anything?" asked Lupin.

"No."

"Neither did I. And yet you notified my aeronaut to prepare the dirigible balloon which will soon carry us into the clouds.

"Come!" said Ganimard, who had completed his search; "we've had enough nonsense—let's be off."

He started away, followed by his men. Lupin did not move. His guardians pushed him in vain.

"Well," said Ganimard, "do you refuse to go?"

"Not at all. But it depends."

"On what?"

"Where you want to take me."

"To the station-house, of course."

"Then I refuse to go. I have no business there."

"Are you crazy?"

"Did I not tell you that I had an important appointment?"

"Lupin!"

"Why, Ganimard, I have an appointment with the blonde Lady, and do you suppose I would be so discourteous as to cause her a moment's anxiety? That would be very ungentlemanly."

"Listen, Lupin," said the detective, who was becoming annoyed by this persiflage; "I have been very patient with you, but I will endure no more. Follow me."

"Impossible; I have an appointment and I shall keep it."

"For the last time—follow me!"

"Impossible!"

At a sign from Ganimard two men seized Lupin by the arms; but they released him at once, uttering cries of pain. Lupin had thrust two long needles into them. The other men now rushed at

Lupin with cries of rage and hatred, eager to avenge their comrades and to avenge themselves for the many affronts he had heaped upon them; and now they struck and beat him to their heart's desire. A violent blow on the temple felled Lupin to the floor.

"If you hurt him you will answer to me," growled Ganimard, in a rage.

He leaned over Lupin to ascertain his condition. Then, learning that he was breathing freely, Ganimard ordered his men to carry the prisoner by the head and feet, while he himself supported the body.

"Go gently, now!... Don't jolt him. Ah! The brutes would have killed him... Well, Lupin, how goes it?"

"None too well, Ganimard... you let them knock me out."

"It was your own fault; you were so obstinate," replied Ganimard. "But I hope they didn't hurt you."

They had left the apartment and were now on the landing. Lupin groaned and stammered:

"Ganimard... the elevator... they are breaking my bones."

"A good idea, an excellent idea," replied Ganimard. "Besides, the stairway is too narrow."

He summoned the elevator. They placed Lupin on the seat with the greatest care. Ganimard took his place beside him and said to his men:

"Go down the stairs and wait for me below. Understand?"

Ganimard closed the door of the elevator. Suddenly the elevator shot upward like a balloon released from its cable. Lupin burst into a fit of sardonic laughter.

"Good God!" cried Ganimard, as he made a frantic search in the dark for the button of descent. Having found it, he cried:

"The fifth floor! Watch the door of the fifth floor."

His assistants clambered up the stairs, two and three steps at a time. But this strange circumstance happened: The elevator seemed to break through the ceiling of the last floor, disappeared from the sight of Ganimard's assistants, suddenly made its appearance on the upper floor—the servants' floor— and stopped. Three men were there waiting for it. They opened the door. Two of them seized Ganimard, who, astonished at the sudden attack, scarcely made any defence. The other man carried off Lupin.

"I warned you, Ganimard... about the dirigible balloon. Another time, don't be so tender-hearted. And, moreover, remember that Arsène Lupin doesn't allow himself to be struck and knocked down without sufficient reason. Adieu."

The door of the elevator was already closed on Ganimard, and the machine began to descend; and it all happened so quickly that the old detective reached the ground floor as soon as his assistants. Without exchanging a word they crossed the court and ascended the servants' stairway, which was the only way to reach the servants' floor through which the escape had been made.

A long corridor with several turns and bordered with little numbered rooms led to a door that was not locked. On the other side of this door and, therefore, in another house there was another corridor with similar turns and similar rooms, and at the end of it a servants' stairway. Ganimard descended it, crossed a court and a vestibule and found himself in the rue Picot. Then he understood the situation: the two houses, built the entire depth of the lots, touched at the rear, while the fronts of the houses faced upon two streets that ran parallel to each other at a distance of more than sixty metres apart.

He found the concierge and, showing his card, enquired:

"Did four men pass here just now?"

"Yes; the two servants from the fourth and fifth floors, with two friends."

"Who lives on the fourth and fifth floors?"

"Two men named Fauvel and their cousins, whose name is Provost. They moved to-day, leaving the two servants, who went away just now."

"Ah!" thought Ganimard; "what a grand opportunity we have missed! The entire band lived in these houses."

And he sank down on a chair in despair.

Forty minutes later two gentlemen were driven up to the station of the Northern Railway and hurried to the Calais express, followed by a porter who carried their valises. One of them had his arm in a sling, and the pallour of his face denoted some illness. The other man was in a jovial mood.

"We must hurry, Wilson, or we will miss the train... Ah! Wilson, I shall never forget these ten days."

"Neither will I."

"Ah! it was a great struggle!"

"Superb!"

"A few repulses, here and there—"

"Of no consequence."

"And, at last, victory all along the line. Lupin arrested! The blue diamond recovered!"

"My arm broken!"

"What does a broken arm count for in such a victory as that?"

"Especially when it is my arm."

"Ah! Yes, don't you remember, Wilson, that it was at the very time you were in the pharmacy, suffering like a hero, that I discovered the clue to the whole mystery?"

"How lucky!"

The doors of the carriages were being closed.

"All aboard. Hurry up, gentlemen!"

The porter climbed into an empty compartment and placed their valises in the rack, whilst Sholmes assisted the unfortunate Wilson.

"What's the matter, Wilson? You're not done up, are you? Come, pull your nerves together."

"My nerves are all right."

"Well, what is it, then?"

"I have only one hand."

"What of it?" exclaimed Sholmes, cheerfully. "You are not the only one who has had a broken arm. Cheer up!"

Sholmes handed the porter a piece of fifty centimes.

"Thank you, Monsieur Sholmes," said the porter.

The Englishman looked at him; it was Arsène Lupin.

"You!... you!" he stammered, absolutely astounded.

And Wilson brandished his sound arm in the manner of a man who demonstrates a fact as he said:

"You! You! But you were arrested! Sholmes told me so. When he left you Ganimard and thirty men had you in charge."

Lupin folded his arms and said, with an air of indignation:

"Did you suppose I would let you go away without bidding you adieu? After the very friendly relations that have always existed between us! That would be discourteous and ungrateful on my part."

The train whistled. Lupin continued:

"I beg your pardon, but have you everything you need? Tobacco and matches... yes... and the evening papers? You will find in them an account of my arrest—your last exploit, Monsieur Sholmes. And now, au revoir. Am delighted to have made your acquaintance. And if ever I can be of any service to you, I shall be only too happy..." He leaped to the platform and closed the door.

"Adieu," he repeated, waving his handkerchief. "Adieu... I shall write to you... You will write also, eh? And your arm broken, Wilson... I am truly sorry... I shall expect to hear from both of you. A postal card, now and then, simply address: Lupin, Paris. That is sufficient... Adieu... See you soon."

Chapter 7

THE JEWISH LAMP

HERLOCK Sholmes and Wilson were sitting in front of the fireplace, in comfortable armchairs, with the feet extended toward the grateful warmth of a glowing coke fire.

Sholmes' pipe, a short brier with a silver band, had gone out. He knocked out the ashes, filled it, lighted it, pulled the skirts of his dressing-gown over his knees, and drew from his pipe great puffs of smoke, which ascended toward the ceiling in scores of shadow rings.

Wilson gazed at him, as a dog lying curled up on a rug before the fire might look at his master, with great round eyes which have no hope other than to obey the least gesture of his owner. Was the master going to break the silence? Would he reveal to Wilson the subject of his reverie and admit his satellite into the charmed realm of his thoughts? When Sholmes had maintained his silent attitude for some time. Wilson ventured to speak:

"Everything seems quiet now. Not the shadow of a case to occupy our leisure moments."

Sholmes did not reply, but the rings of smoke emitted by Sholmes were better formed, and Wilson observed that his companion drew considerable pleasure from that trifling fact— an indication that the great man was not absorbed in any serious meditation. Wilson, discouraged, arose and went to the window.

The lonely street extended between the gloomy façades of grimy houses, unusually gloomy this morning by reason of a heavy downfall of rain. A cab passed; then another. Wilson made an entry of their numbers in his memorandum-book. One never knows!

"Ah!" he exclaimed, "the postman."

The man entered, shown in by the servant.

"Two registered letters, sir... if you will sign, please?"

Sholmes signed the receipts, accompanied the man to the door, and was opening one of the letters as he returned.

"It seems to please you," remarked Wilson, after a moment's silence.

"This letter contains a very interesting proposition. You are anxious for a case—here's one. Read—"

Wilson read:

"Monsieur,

"I desire the benefit of your services and experience. I have been the victim of a serious theft, and the investigation has as yet been unsuccessful. I am sending to you by this mail a number of newspapers which will inform you of the affair, and if you will undertake the case, I will place my house at your disposal and ask you to fill in the enclosed check, signed by me, for whatever sum you require for your expenses.

"Kindly reply by telegraph, and much oblige,

"Your humble servant,

"Baron Victor d'Imblevalle,

"18 rue Murillo, Paris."

"Ah!" exclaimed Sholmes, "that sounds good... a little trip to Paris... and why not, Wilson? Since my famous duel with Arsène Lupin, I have not had an excuse to go there. I should be pleased to visit the capital of the world under less strenuous conditions."

He tore the check into four pieces and, while Wilson, whose arm had not yet regained its former strength, uttered bitter words against Paris and the Parisians, Sholmes opened the second envelope. Immediately, he made a gesture of annoyance, and a wrinkle appeared on his forehead during the reading of the letter; then, crushing the paper into a ball, he threw it, angrily, on the floor.

"Well? What's the matter?" asked Wilson, anxiously.

He picked up the ball of paper, unfolded it, and read, with increasing amazement:

> "My Dear Monsieur:
>
> "You know full well the admiration I have for you and the interest I take in your renown. Well, believe me, when I warn you to have nothing whatever to do with the case on which you have just now been called to Paris. Your intervention will cause much harm; your efforts will produce a most lamentable result; and you will be obliged to make a public confession of your defeat.
>
> "Having a sincere desire to spare you such humiliation, I implore you, in the name of the friendship that unites us, to remain peacefully reposing at your own fireside.
>
> "My best wishes to Monsieur Wilson, and, for yourself, the sincere regards of your devoted ARSÈNE LUPIN."

"Arsène Lupin!" repeated Wilson, astounded.

Sholmes struck the table with his fist, and exclaimed:

"Ah! He is pestering me already, the fool! He laughs at me as if I were a schoolboy! The public confession of my defeat! Didn't I force him to disgorge the blue diamond?"

"I tell you—he's afraid," suggested Wilson.

"Nonsense! Arsène Lupin is not afraid, and this taunting letter proves it."

"But how did he know that the Baron d'Imblevalle had written to you?"

"What do I know about it? You do ask some stupid questions, my boy."

"I thought... I supposed—"

"What? That I am a clairvoyant? Or a sorcerer?"

"No, but I have seen you do some marvellous things."

"No person can perform *marvellous* things. I no more than you. I reflect, I deduct, I conclude—that is all; but I do not divine. Only fools divine."

Wilson assumed the attitude of a whipped cur, and resolved not to make a fool of himself by trying to divine why Sholmes paced the room with quick, nervous strides. But when Sholmes rang for the servant and ordered his valise, Wilson thought that he was in possession of a material fact which gave him the right to reflect, deduct and conclude that his associate was about to take a journey. The same mental operation permitted him to assert, with almost mathematical exactness:

"Sholmes, you are going to Paris."

"Possibly."

"And Lupin's affront impels you to go, rather than the desire to assist the Baron d'Imblevalle."

"Possibly."

"Sholmes, I shall go with you."

"Ah; ah! my old friend," exclaimed Sholmes, interrupting his walking, "you are not afraid that your right arm will meet the same fate as your left?"

"What can happen to me? You will be there."

"That's the way to talk, Wilson. We will show that clever Frenchman that he made a mistake when he threw his glove in our faces. Be quick, Wilson, we must catch the first train."

"Without waiting for the papers the baron has sent you?"

"What good are they?"

"I will send a telegram."

"No; if you do that, Arsène Lupin will know of my arrival. I wish to avoid that. This time, Wilson, we must fight under cover."

That afternoon, the two friends embarked at Dover. The passage was a delightful one. In the train from Calais to Paris, Sholmes had three hours sound sleep, while Wilson guarded the door of the compartment.

Sholmes awoke in good spirits. He was delighted at the idea of another duel with Arsène Lupin, and he rubbed his hands with the satisfied air of a man who looks forward to a pleasant vacation.

"At last!" exclaimed Wilson, "we are getting to work again."

And he rubbed his hands with the same satisfied air.

At the station, Sholmes took the wraps and, followed by Wilson, who carried the valises, he gave up his tickets and started off briskly.

"Fine weather, Wilson... Blue sky and sunshine! Paris is giving us a royal reception."

"Yes, but what a crowd!"

"So much the better, Wilson, we will pass unnoticed. No one will recognize us in such a crowd."

"Is this Monsieur Sholmes?"

He stopped, somewhat puzzled. Who the deuce could thus address him by his name? A woman stood beside him; a young girl whose simple dress outlined her slender form and whose pretty face had a sad and anxious expression. She repeated her enquiry:

"You are Monsieur Sholmes?"

As he still remained silent, as much from confusion as from a habit of prudence, the girl asked a third time:

"Have I the honour of addressing Monsieur Sholmes?"

"What do you want?" he replied, testily, considering the incident a suspicious one.

"You must listen to me, Monsieur Sholmes, as it is a serious matter. I know that you are going to the rue Murillo."

"What do you say?"

"I know... I know... rue Murillo... number 18. Well, you must not go... no, you must not. I assure you that you will regret it. Do not think that I have any interest in the matter. I do it because it is right... because my conscience tells me to do it."

Sholmes tried to get away, but she persisted:

"Oh! I beg of you, don't neglect my advice... Ah! if I only knew how to convince you! Look at me! Look into my eyes! They are sincere ... they speak the truth."

She gazed at Sholmes, fearlessly but innocently, with those beautiful eyes, serious and clear, in which her very soul seemed to be reflected.

Wilson nodded his head, as he said:

"Mademoiselle looks honest."

"Yes," she implored, "and you must have confidence——"

"I have confidence in you, mademoiselle," replied Wilson.

"Oh, how happy you make me! And so has your friend? I feel it ... I am sure of it! What happiness! Everything will be all right now!... What a good idea of mine!... Ah! yes, there is a train for Calais in twenty minutes. You will take it... Quick, follow me... you must come this way... there is just time."

She tried to drag them along. Sholmes seized her arm, and in as gentle a voice as he could assume, said to her:

"Excuse me, mademoiselle, if I cannot yield to your wishes, but I never abandon a task that I have once undertaken."

"I beseech you... I implore you... Ah if you could only understand!"

Sholmes passed outside and walked away at a quick pace. Wilson said to the girl:

"Have no fear... he will be in at the finish. He never failed yet."

And he ran to overtake Sholmes.

HERLOCK SHOLMES—ARSÈNE LUPIN.

These words, in great black letters, met their gaze as soon as they left the railway station. A number of sandwich-men were parading through the street, one behind the other, carrying heavy canes with iron ferrules with which they struck the pavement in harmony, and, on their backs, they carried large posters, on which one could read the following notice:

THE MATCH BETWEEN HERLOCK SHOLMES AND ARSÈNE LUPIN. ARRIVAL OF THE ENGLISH CHAMPION. THE GREAT DETECTIVE ATTACKS THE MYSTERY OF THE RUE MURILLO. READ THE DETAILS IN THE "ECHO DE FRANCE".

Wilson shook his head, and said:

"Look at that, Sholmes, and we thought we were traveling incognito! I shouldn't be surprised to find the republican guard waiting for us at the rue Murillo to give us an official reception with toasts and champagne."

"Wilson, when you get funny, you get beastly funny," growled Sholmes.

Then he approached one of the sandwich-men with the obvious intention of seizing him in his powerful grip and crushing him, together with his infernal sign-board. There was quite a crowd gathered about the men, reading the notices, and joking and laughing.

Repressing a furious access of rage, Sholmes said to the man:

"When did they hire you?"

"This morning."

"How long have you been parading?"

"About an hour."

"But the boards were ready before that?"

"Oh, yes, they were ready when we went to the agency this morning."

So then it appears that Arsène Lupin had foreseen that he, Sholmes, would accept the challenge. More than that, the letter written by Lupin showed that he was eager for the fray and that he was prepared to measure swords once more with his formidable rival. Why? What motive could Arsène Lupin have in renewing the struggle?

Sholmes hesitated for a moment. Lupin must be very confident of his success to show so much insolence in advance; and was not he, Sholmes, falling into a trap by rushing into the battle at the first call for help?

However, he called a carriage.

"Come, Wilson!... Driver, 18 rue Murillo!" he exclaimed, with an outburst of his accustomed energy. With distended veins and clenched fists, as if he were about to engage in a boxing bout, he jumped into the carriage.

The rue Murillo is bordered with magnificent private residences, the rear of which overlook the Parc Monceau. One of the most pretentious of these houses is number 18, owned and occupied by the Baron d'Imblevalle and furnished in a luxurious manner consistent with the owner's taste and wealth. There was a courtyard in front of the house, and, in the rear, a garden well filled with trees whose branches mingle with those of the park.

After ringing the bell, the two Englishmen were admitted, crossed the courtyard, and were received at the door by a footman who showed them into a small parlour facing the garden in the rear of the house. They sat down and, glancing about, made a rapid inspection of the many valuable objects with which the room was filled.

"Everything very choice," murmured Wilson, "and in the best of taste. It is a safe deduction to make that those who had the leisure to collect these articles must now be at least fifty years of age."

The door opened, and the Baron d'Imblevalle entered, followed by his wife. Contrary to the deduction made by Wilson, they were both quite young, of elegant appearance, and vivacious in speech and action. They were profuse in their expressions of gratitude.

"So kind of you to come! Sorry to have caused you so much trouble! The theft now seems of little consequence, since it has procured us this pleasure."

"How charming these French people are!" thought Wilson, evolving one of his commonplace deductions.

"But time is money," exclaimed the baron, "especially your time, Monsieur Sholmes. So I will come to the point. Now, what do you think of the affair? Do you think you can succeed in it?"

"Before I can answer that I must know what it is about."

"I thought you knew."

"No; so I must ask you for full particulars, even to the smallest detail. First, what is the nature of the case?"

"A theft."

"When did it take place?"

"Last Saturday," replied the baron, "or, at least, sometime during Saturday night or Sunday morning."

"That was six days ago. Now, you can tell me all about it."

"In the first place, monsieur, I must tell you that my wife and I, conforming to the manner of life that our position demands, go out very little. The education of our children, a few receptions, and the care and decoration of our house—such constitutes our life; and nearly all our evenings are spent in this little room, which is my wife's boudoir, and in which we have gathered a few artistic objects. Last Saturday night, about eleven o'clock, I turned off the electric lights, and my wife and I retired, as usual, to our room."

"Where is your room?"

"It adjoins this. That is the door. Next morning, that is to say, Sunday morning, I arose quite early. As Suzanne, my wife, was still asleep, I passed into the boudoir as quietly as possible so as not to wake her. What was my astonishment when I found that window open—as we had left it closed the evening before!"

"A servant—"

"No one enters here in the morning until we ring. Besides, I always take the precaution to bolt the second door which communicates with the ante-chamber. Therefore, the window must have been opened from the outside. Besides, I have some evidence of that: the second pane of glass from the right—close to the fastening—had been cut."

"And what does that window overlook?"

"As you can see for yourself, it opens on a little balcony, surrounded by a stone railing. Here, we are on the first floor, and you can see the garden behind the house and the iron fence which separates it from the Parc Monceau. It is quite certain that the thief came through the park, climbed the fence by the aid of a ladder, and thus reached the terrace below the window."

"That is quite certain, you say!"

"Well, in the soft earth on either side of the fence, they found the two holes made by the bottom of the ladder, and two similar holes can be seen below the window. And the stone railing of the balcony shows two scratches which were doubtless made by the contact of the ladder."

"Is the Parc Monceau closed at night?"

"No; but if it were, there is a house in course of erection at number 14, and a person could enter that way."

Herlock Sholmes reflected for a few minutes, and then said:

"Let us come down to the theft. It must have been committed in this room?"

"Yes; there was here, between that twelfth century Virgin and that tabernacle of chased silver, a small Jewish lamp. It has disappeared."

"And is that all?"

"That is all."

"Ah!... And what is a Jewish lamp?"

"One of those copper lamps used by the ancient Jews, consisting of a standard which supported a bowl containing the oil, and from this bowl projected several burners intended for the wicks."

"Upon the whole, an object of small value."

"No great value, of course. But this one contained a secret hiding-place in which we were accustomed to place a magnificent jewel, a chimera in gold, set with rubies and emeralds, which was of great value."

"Why did you hide it there?"

"Oh! I can't give any reason, monsieur, unless it was an odd fancy to utilize a hiding-place of that kind."

"Did anyone know it?"

"No."

"No one—except the thief," said Sholmes. "Otherwise he would not have taken the trouble to steal the lamp."

"Of course. But how could he know it, as it was only by accident that the secret mechanism of the lamp was revealed to us."

"A similar accident has revealed it to someone else... a servant... or an acquaintance. But let us proceed: I suppose the police have been notified?"

"Yes. The examining magistrate has completed his investigation. The reporter-detectives attached to the leading newspapers have also made their investigations. But, as I wrote to you, it seems to me the mystery will never be solved."

Sholmes arose, went to the window, examined the casement, the balcony, the terrace, studied the scratches on the stone railing with his magnifying-glass, and then requested Mon. d'Imblevalle to show him the garden.

Outside, Sholmes sat down in a rattan chair and gazed at the roof of the house in a dreamy way. Then he walked over to the two little wooden boxes with which they had covered the holes made in the ground by the bottom of the ladder with a view of preserving them intact. He raised the boxes, kneeled on the ground, scrutinized the holes and made some measurements. After making a similar examination of the holes near the fence, he and the baron returned to the boudoir where Madame d'Imblevalle was waiting for them. After a short silence Sholmes said:

"At the very outset of your story, baron, I was surprised at the very simple methods employed by the thief. To raise a ladder, cut a window-pane, select a valuable article, and walk out again— no, that is not the way such things are done. All that is too plain, too simple."

"Well, what do you think?"

"That the Jewish lamp was stolen under the direction of Arsène Lupin."

"Arsène Lupin!" exclaimed the baron.

"Yes, but he did not do it himself, as no one came from the outside. Perhaps a servant descended from the upper floor by means of a waterspout that I noticed when I was in the garden."

"What makes you think so?"

"Arsène Lupin would not leave this room empty-handed."

"Empty-handed! But he had the lamp."

"But that would not have prevented his taking that snuff-box, set with diamonds, or that opal necklace. When he leaves anything, it is because he can't carry it away."

"But the marks of the ladder outside?"

"A false scent. Placed there simply to avert suspicion."

"And the scratches on the balustrade?"

"A farce! They were made with a piece of sandpaper. See, here are scraps of the paper that I picked up in the garden."

"And what about the marks made by the bottom of the ladder?"

"Counterfeit! Examine the two rectangular holes below the window, and the two holes near the fence. They are of a similar form, but I find that the two holes near the house are closer to each other than the two holes near the fence. What does that fact suggest? To me, it suggested that the four holes were made by a piece of wood prepared for the purpose."

"The better proof would be the piece of wood itself."

"Here it is," said Sholmes, "I found it in the garden, under the box of a laurel tree."

The baron bowed to Sholmes in recognition of his skill. Only forty minutes had elapsed since the Englishman had entered the house, and he had already exploded all the theories theretofore formed, and which had been based on what appeared to be obvious and undeniable facts. But what now appeared to be the real facts of the case rested upon a more solid foundation, to-wit, the astute reasoning of a Herlock Sholmes.

"The accusation which you make against one of our household is a very serious matter," said the baroness. "Our servants have been with us a long time and none of them would betray our trust."

"If none of them has betrayed you, how can you explain the fact that I received this letter on the same day and by the same mail as the letter you wrote to me?"

He handed to the baroness the letter that he had received from Arsène Lupin. She exclaimed, in amazement:

"Arsène Lupin! How could he know?"

"Did you tell anyone that you had written to me?"

"No one," replied the baron. "The idea occurred to us the other evening at the dinner-table."

"Before the servants?"

"No, only our two children. Oh, no... Sophie and Henriette had left the table, hadn't they, Suzanne?"

Madame d'Imblevalle, after a moment's reflection, replied:

"Yes, they had gone to Mademoiselle."

"Mademoiselle?" queried Sholmes.

"The governess, Mademoiselle Alice Demun."

"Does she take her meals with you?"

"No. Her meals are served in her room."

Wilson had an idea. He said:

"The letter written to my friend Herlock Sholmes was posted?"

"Of course."

"Who posted it?"

"Dominique, who has been my valet for twenty years," replied the baron. "Any search in that direction would be a waste of time."

"One never wastes his time when engaged in a search," said Wilson, sententiously.

This preliminary investigation now ended, and Sholmes asked permission to retire.

At dinner, an hour later, he saw Sophie and Henriette, the two children of the family, one was six and the other eight years of age. There was very little conversation at the table. Sholmes responded to the friendly advances of his hosts in such a curt manner that they were soon reduced to silence. When the coffee was served, Sholmes swallowed the contents of his cup, and rose to take his leave.

At that moment, a servant entered with a telephone message addressed to Sholmes. He opened it, and read:

> "You have my enthusiastic admiration. The results attained by you in so short a time are simply marvellous. I am dismayed.
>
> "ARSÈNE LUPIN."

Sholmes made a gesture of indignation and handed the message to the baron, saying:

"What do you think now, monsieur? Are the walls of your house furnished with eyes and ears?"

"I don't understand it," said the baron, in amazement.

"Nor do I; but I do understand that Lupin has knowledge of everything that occurs in this house. He knows every movement, every word. There is no doubt of it. But how does he get his information? That is the first mystery I have to solve, and when I know that I will know everything."

That night, Wilson retired with the clear conscience of a man who has performed his whole duty and thus acquired an undoubted right to sleep and repose. So he fell asleep very quickly, and was soon enjoying the most delightful dreams in which he pursued Lupin and captured him single-handed; and the sensation was so vivid and exciting that it woke him from his sleep. Someone was standing at his bedside. He seized his revolver, and cried:

"Don't move, Lupin, or I'll fire."

"The deuce! Wilson, what do you mean?"

"Oh! It is you, Sholmes. Do you want me?"

"I want to show you something. Get up."

Sholmes led him to the window, and said:

"Look!... On the other side of the fence..."

"In the park?"

"Yes. What do you see?"

"I don't see anything."

"Yes, you do see something."

"Ah! Of course, a shadow... two of them."

"Yes, close to the fence. See, they are moving. Come, quick!"

Quickly they descended the stairs, and reached a room which opened into the garden. Through the glass door they could see the two shadowy forms in the same place.

"It is very strange," said Sholmes, "but it seems to me I can hear a noise inside the house."

"Inside the house? Impossible! Everybody is asleep."

"Well, listen—"

At that moment a low whistle came from the other side of the fence, and they perceived a dim light which appeared to come from the house.

"The baron must have turned on the light in his room. It is just above us."

"That must have been the noise you heard," said Wilson. "Perhaps they are watching the fence also."

Then there was a second whistle, softer than before.

"I don't understand it; I don't understand," said Sholmes, irritably.

"No more do I," confessed Wilson.

Sholmes turned the key, drew the bolt, and quietly opened the door. A third whistle, louder than before, and modulated to another form. And the noise above their heads became more pronounced. Sholmes said:

"It seems to be on the balcony outside the boudoir window."

He put his head through the half-opened door, but immediately recoiled, with a stifled oath. Then Wilson looked. Quite close to them there was a ladder, the upper end of which was resting on the balcony.

"The deuce!" said Sholmes, "there is someone in the boudoir. That is what we heard. Quick, let us remove the ladder."

But at that instant a man slid down the ladder and ran toward the spot where his accomplices were waiting for him outside the fence. He carried the ladder with him. Sholmes and Wilson pursued the man and overtook him just as he was placing the ladder against the fence. From the other side of the fence two shots were fired.

"Wounded?" cried Sholmes.

"No," replied Wilson.

Wilson seized the man by the body and tried to hold him, but the man turned and plunged a knife into Wilson's breast. He uttered a groan, staggered and fell.

"Damnation!" muttered Sholmes, "if they have killed him I will kill them."

He laid Wilson on the grass and rushed toward the ladder. Too late—the man had climbed the fence and, accompanied by his confederates, had fled through the bushes.

"Wilson, Wilson, it is not serious, hein? Merely a scratch."

The house door opened, and Monsieur d'Imblevalle appeared, followed by the servants, carrying candles.

"What's the matter?" asked the baron. "Is Monsieur Wilson wounded?"

"Oh! It's nothing—a mere scratch," repeated Sholmes, trying to deceive himself.

The blood was flowing profusely, and Wilson's face was livid. Twenty minutes later the doctor ascertained that the point of the knife had penetrated to within an inch and a half of the heart.

"An inch and a half of the heart! Wilson always was lucky!" said Sholmes, in an envious tone.

"Lucky... lucky..." muttered the doctor.

"Of course! Why, with his robust constitution he will soon be out again."

"Six weeks in bed and two months of convalescence."

"Not more?"

"No, unless complications set in."

"Oh! The devil! What does he want complications for?"

Fully reassured, Sholmes joined the baron in the boudoir. This time the mysterious visitor had not exercised the same restraint. Ruthlessly, he had laid his vicious hand upon the diamond snuff-box, upon the opal necklace, and, in a general way, upon everything that could find a place in the greedy pockets of an enterprising burglar.

The window was still open; one of the window-panes had been neatly cut; and, in the morning, a summary investigation showed that the ladder belonged to the house then in course of construction.

"Now, you can see," said Mon. d'Imblevalle, with a touch of irony, "it is an exact repetition of the affair of the Jewish lamp."

"Yes, if we accept the first theory adopted by the police."

"Haven't you adopted it yet? Doesn't this second theft shatter your theory in regard to the first?"

"It only confirms it, monsieur."

"That is incredible! You have positive evidence that last night's theft was committed by an outsider, and yet you adhere to your theory that the Jewish lamp was stolen by someone in the house."

"Yes, I am sure of it."

"How do you explain it?"

"I do not explain anything, monsieur; I have established two facts which do not appear to have any relation to each other, and yet I am seeking the missing link that connects them."

His conviction seemed to be so earnest and positive that the baron submitted to it, and said:

"Very well, we will notify the police—"

"Not at all!" exclaimed the Englishman, quickly, "not at all! I intend to ask for their assistance when I need it—but not before."

"But the attack on your friend?"

"That's of no consequence. He is only wounded. Secure the licence of the doctor. I shall be responsible for the legal side of the affair."

The next two days proved uneventful. Yet Sholmes was investigating the case with minute care, and with a sense of wounded pride resulting from that audacious theft, committed under his nose, in spite of his presence and beyond his power to prevent it. He made a thorough investigation of the house and garden, interviewed the servants, and paid lengthy visits to the kitchen and stables. And, although his efforts were fruitless, he did not despair.

"I will succeed," he thought, "and the solution must be sought within the walls of this house. This affair is quite different from that of the blonde Lady, where I had to work in the dark, on unknown ground. This time I am on the battlefield itself. The enemy is not the elusive and invisible Lupin, but the accomplice, in flesh and blood, who lives and moves within the confines of this house. Let me secure the slightest clue and the game is mine!"

That clue was furnished to him by accident.

On the afternoon of the third day, when he entered a room located above the boudoir, which served as a study for the children, he found Henriette, the younger of the two sisters. She was looking for her scissors.

"You know," she said to Sholmes, "I make papers like that you received the other evening."

"The other evening?"

"Yes, just as dinner was over, you received a paper with marks on it... you know, a telegram... Well, I make them, too."

She left the room. To anyone else these words would seem to be nothing more than the insignificant remark of a child, and Sholmes himself listened to them with a distracted air and continued his investigation. But, suddenly, he ran after the child, and overtook her at the head of the stairs. He said to her:

"So you paste stamps and marks on papers?"

Henriette, very proudly, replied:

"Yes, I cut them out and paste them on."

"Who taught you that little game?"

"Mademoiselle... my governess... I have seen her do it often. She takes words out of the newspapers and pastes them—"

"What does she make out of them?"

"Telegrams and letters that she sends away."

Herlock Sholmes returned to the study, greatly puzzled by the information and seeking to draw from it a logical deduction. There was a pile of newspapers on the mantel. He opened them and found that many words and, in some places, entire lines had been cut out. But, after reading a few of the word's which preceded or followed, he decided that the missing words had been cut out at random—probably by the child. It was possible that one of the newspapers had been cut by mademoiselle; but how could he assure himself that such was the case?

Mechanically, Sholmes turned over the school-books on the table; then others which were lying on the shelf of a bookcase. Suddenly he uttered a cry of joy. In a corner of the bookcase, under a pile of old exercise books, he found a child's alphabet-book, in which the letters were ornamented with pictures, and on one of the pages of that book he discovered a place where a word had been removed. He examined it. It was a list of the days of the week. Monday, Tuesday, Wednesday, etc. The word "Saturday" was missing. Now, the theft of the Jewish lamp had occurred on a Saturday night.

Sholmes experienced that slight fluttering of the heart which always announced to him, in the clearest manner, that he had discovered the road which leads to victory. That ray of truth, that feeling of certainty, never deceived him.

With nervous fingers he hastened to examine the balance of the book. Very soon he made another discovery. It was a page composed of capital letters, followed by a line of figures. Nine of those letters and three of those figures had been carefully cut out. Sholmes made a list of the missing letters and figures in his memorandum book, in alphabetical and numerical order, and obtained the following result:

CDEHNOPEZ—237.

"Well? at first sight, it is a rather formidable puzzle," he murmured, "but, by transposing the letters and using all of them, is it possible to form one, two or three complete words?"

Sholmes tried it, in vain.

Only one solution seemed possible; it constantly appeared before him, no matter which way he tried to juggle the letters, until, at length, he was satisfied it was the true solution, since it harmonized with the logic of the facts and the general circumstances of the case.

As that page of the book did not contain any duplicate letters it was probable, in fact quite certain, that the words he could form from those letters would be incomplete, and that the original words had been completed with letters taken from other pages. Under those conditions he obtained the following solution, errors and omissions excepted:

REPOND Z—CH—237.

The first word was quite clear: répondez [reply], a letter E is missing because it occurs twice in the word, and the book furnished only one letter of each kind.

As to the second incomplete word, no doubt it formed, with the aid of the number 237, an address to which the reply was to be sent. They appointed Saturday as the time, and requested a reply to be sent to the address CH. 237.

Or, perhaps, CH. 237 was an address for a letter to be sent to the "general delivery" of some post office, or, again, they might form a part of some incomplete word. Sholmes searched the book once more, but did not discover that any other letters had been removed. Therefore, until further orders, he decided to adhere to the foregoing interpretation.

Henriette returned and observed what he was doing.

"Amusing, isn't it?"

"Yes, very amusing," he replied. "But, have you any other papers?... Or, rather, words already cut out that I can paste?"

"Papers?... No... And Mademoiselle wouldn't like it."

"Mademoiselle?"

"Yes, she has scolded me already."

"Why?"

"Because I have told you some things... and she says that a person should never tell things about those they love."

"You are quite right."

Henriette was delighted to receive his approbation, in fact so highly pleased that she took from a little silk bag that was pinned to her dress some scraps of cloth, three buttons, two cubes of sugar and, lastly, a piece of paper which she handed to Sholmes.

"See, I give it to you just the same."

It was the number of a cab—8,279.

"Where did this number come from?"

"It fell out of her pocketbook."

"When?"

"Sunday, at mass, when she was taking out some sous for the collection."

"Exactly! And now I shall tell you how to keep from being scolded again. Do not tell Mademoiselle that you saw me."

Sholmes then went to Mon. d'Imblevalle and questioned him in regard to Mademoiselle. The baron replied, indignantly:

"Alice Demun! How can you imagine such a thing? It is utterly impossible!"

"How long has she been in your service?"

"Only a year, but there is no one in the house in whom I have greater confidence."

"Why have I not seen her yet?"

"She has been away for a few days."

"But she is here now."

"Yes; since her return she has been watching at the bedside of your friend. She has all the qualities of a nurse... gentle... thoughtful... Monsieur Wilson seems much pleased..."

"Ah!" said Sholmes, who had completely neglected to inquire about his friend. After a moment's reflection he asked:

"Did she go out on Sunday morning?"

"The day after the theft?"

"Yes."

The baron called his wife and asked her. She replied:

"Mademoiselle went to the eleven o'clock mass with the children, as usual."

"But before that?"

"Before that? No... Let me see!... I was so upset by the theft... but I remember now that, on the evening before, she asked permission to go out on Sunday morning... to see a cousin who was passing through Paris, I think. But, surely, you don't suspect her?"

"Of course not... but I would like to see her."

He went to Wilson's room. A woman dressed in a gray cloth dress, as in the hospitals, was bending over the invalid, giving him a drink. When she turned her face Sholmes recognized her as the young girl who had accosted him at the railway station.

Alice Demun smiled sweetly; her great serious, innocent eyes showed no sign of embarrassment. The Englishman tried to speak, muttered a few syllables, and stopped. Then she resumed her work, acting quite naturally under Sholmes' astonished gaze, moved the bottles, unrolled and rolled cotton bandages, and again regarded Sholmes with her charming smile of pure innocence.

He turned on his heels, descended the stairs, noticed Mon. d'Imblevalle's automobile in the courtyard, jumped into it, and went to Levallois, to the office of the cab company whose address was printed on the paper he had received from Henriette. The man who had driven carriage number 8,279 on Sunday morning not being there, Sholmes dismissed the automobile and waited for the man's return. He told Sholmes that he had picked up a woman in the vicinity of the Parc Monceau, a young woman dressed in black, wearing a heavy veil, and, apparently, quite nervous.

"Did she have a package?"

"Yes, quite a long package."

"Where did you take her?"

"Avenue des Ternes, corner of the Place Saint-Ferdinand. She remained there about ten minutes, and then returned to the Parc Monceau."

"Could you recognize the house in the avenue des Ternes?"

"Parbleu! Shall I take you there?"

"Presently. First take me to 36 quai des Orfèvres."

At the police office he saw Detective Ganimard.

"Monsieur Ganimard, are you at liberty?"

"If it has anything to do with Lupin—no!"

"It has something to do with Lupin."

"Then I do not go."

"What! you surrender—"

"I bow to the inevitable. I am tired of the unequal struggle, in which we are sure to be defeated. Lupin is stronger than I am—stronger than the two of us; therefore, we must surrender."

"I will not surrender."

"He will make you, as he has all others."

"And you would be pleased to see it—eh, Ganimard?"

"At all events, it is true," said Ganimard, frankly. "And since you are determined to pursue the game, I will go with you."

Together they entered the carriage and were driven to the avenue des Ternes. Upon their order the carriage stopped on the other side of the street, at some distance from the house, in front of a little café, on the terrace of which the two men took seats amongst the shrubbery. It was commencing to grow dark.

"Waiter," said Sholmes, "some writing material."

He wrote a note, recalled the waiter and gave him the letter with instructions to deliver it to the concierge of the house which he pointed out.

In a few minutes the concierge stood before them. Sholmes asked him if, on the Sunday morning, he had seen a young woman dressed in black.

"In black? Yes, about nine o'clock. She went to the second floor."

"Have you seen her often?"

"No, but for some time—well, during the last few weeks, I have seen her almost every day."

"And since Sunday?"

"Only once... until to-day."

"What! Did she come today?"

"She is here now."

"Here now?"

"Yes, she came about ten minutes ago. Her carriage is standing in the Place Saint-Ferdinand, as usual. I met her at the door."

"Who is the occupant of the second floor?"

"There are two: a modiste, Mademoiselle Langeais, and a gentleman who rented two furnished rooms a month ago under the name of Bresson."

"Why do you say 'under the name'?"

"Because I have an idea that it is an assumed name. My wife takes care of his rooms, and ... well, there are not two shirts there with the same initials."

"Is he there much of the time?"

"No; he is nearly always out. He has not been here for three days."

"Was he here on Saturday night?"

"Saturday night?... Let me think... Yes, Saturday night, he came in and stayed all night."

"What sort of a man is he?"

"Well, I can scarcely answer that. He is so changeable. He is, by turns, big, little, fat, thin ... dark and light. I do not always recognize him."

Ganimard and Sholmes exchanged looks.

"That is he, all right," said Ganimard.

"Ah!" said the concierge, "there is the girl now."

Mademoiselle had just emerged from the house and was walking toward her carriage in the Place Saint-Ferdinand.

"And there is Monsieur Bresson."

"Monsieur Bresson? Which is he?"

"The man with the parcel under his arm."

"But he is not looking after the girl. She is going to her carriage alone."

"Yes, I have never seen them together."

The two detectives had arisen. By the light of the street-lamps they recognized the form of Arsène Lupin, who had started off in a direction opposite to that taken by the girl.

"Which will you follow?" asked Ganimard.

"I will follow him, of course. He's the biggest game."

"Then I will follow the girl," proposed Ganimard.

"No, no," said Sholmes, quickly, who did not wish to disclose the girl's identity to Ganimard, "I know where to find her. Come with me."

They followed Lupin at a safe distance, taking care to conceal themselves as well as possible amongst the moving throng and behind the newspaper kiosks. They found the pursuit an easy one, as he walked steadily forward without turning to the right or left, but with a slight limp in the right leg, so slight as to require the keen eye of a professional observer to detect it. Ganimard observed it, and said:

"He is pretending to be lame. Ah! if we could only collect two or three policemen and pounce on our man! We run a chance to lose him."

But they did not meet any policemen before they reached the Porte des Ternes, and, having passed the fortifications, there was no prospect of receiving any assistance.

"We had better separate," said Sholmes, "as there are so few people on the street."

They were now on the Boulevard Victor-Hugo. They walked one on each side of the street, and kept well in the shadow of the trees. They continued thus for twenty minutes, when Lupin turned to the left and followed the Seine. Very soon they saw him descend to the edge of the river. He remained there only a few seconds, but they could not observe his movements. Then Lupin retraced his steps. His pursuers concealed themselves in the shadow of a gateway. Lupin passed in front of them. His parcel had disappeared. And as he walked away another man emerged from the shelter of a house and glided amongst the trees.

"He seems to be following him also," said Sholmes, in a low voice.

The pursuit continued, but was now embarrassed by the presence of the third man. Lupin returned the same way, passed through the Porte des Ternes, and re-entered the house in the avenue des Ternes.

The concierge was closing the house for the night when Ganimard presented himself.

"Did you see him?"

"Yes," replied the concierge, "I was putting out the gas on the landing when he closed and bolted his door."

"Is there any person with him?"

"No; he has no servant. He never eats here."

"Is there a servants' stairway?"

"No."

Ganimard said to Sholmes:

"I had better stand at the door of his room while you go for the commissary of police in the rue Demours."

"And if he should escape during that time?" said Sholmes.

"While I am here! He can't escape."

"One to one, with Lupin, is not an even chance for you."

"Well, I can't force the door. I have no right to do that, especially at night."

Sholmes shrugged his shoulders and said:

"When you arrest Lupin no one will question the methods by which you made the arrest. However, let us go up and ring, and see what happens then."

They ascended to the second floor. There was a double door at the left of the landing. Ganimard rang the bell. No reply. He rang again. Still no reply.

"Let us go in," said Sholmes.

"All right, come on," replied Ganimard.

Yet, they stood still, irresolute. Like people who hesitate when they ought to accomplish a decisive action they feared to move, and it seemed to them impossible that Arsène Lupin was there, so close to them, on the other side of that fragile door that could be broken down by one blow of the fist. But they knew Lupin too well to suppose that he would allow himself to be trapped in that stupid manner. No, no—a thousand times, no—Lupin was no longer there. Through the adjoining houses, over the roofs, by some conveniently prepared exit, he must have already made his escape, and, once more, it would only be Lupin's shadow that they would seize.

They shuddered as a slight noise, coming from the other side of the door, reached their ears. Then they had the impression, amounting almost to a certainty, that he was there, separated from them by that frail wooden door, and that he was listening to them, that he could hear them.

What was to be done? The situation was a serious one. In spite of their vast experience as detectives, they were so nervous and excited that they thought they could hear the beating of their own hearts. Ganimard questioned Sholmes by a look. Then he struck the door a violent blow with his fist. Immediately they heard the sound of footsteps, concerning which there was no attempt at concealment.

Ganimard shook the door. Then he and Sholmes, uniting their efforts, rushed at the door, and burst it open with their shoulders. Then they stood still, in surprise. A shot had been fired in the adjoining room. Another shot, and the sound of a falling body.

When they entered they saw the man lying on the floor with his face toward the marble mantel. His revolver had fallen from his hand. Ganimard stooped and turned the man's head. The face was covered with blood, which was flowing from two wounds, one in the cheek, the other in the temple.

"You can't recognize him for blood."

"No matter!" said Sholmes. "It is not Lupin."

"How do you know? You haven't even looked at him."

"Do you think that Arsène Lupin is the kind of a man that would kill himself?" asked Sholmes, with a sneer.

"But we thought we recognized him outside."

"We thought so, because the wish was father to the thought. That man has us bewitched."

"Then it must be one of his accomplices."

"The accomplices of Arsène Lupin do not kill themselves."

"Well, then, who is it?"

They searched the corpse. In one pocket Herlock Sholmes found an empty pocketbook; in another Ganimard found several louis. There were no marks of identification on any part of his clothing. In a trunk and two valises they found nothing but wearing apparel. On the mantel there was a pile of newspapers. Ganimard opened them. All of them contained articles referring to the theft of the Jewish lamp.

An hour later, when Ganimard and Sholmes left the house, they had acquired no further knowledge of the strange individual who had been driven to suicide by their untimely visit.

Who was he? Why had he killed himself? What was his connection with the affair of the Jewish lamp? Who had followed him on his return from the river? The situation involved many complex questions—many mysteries——

Herlock Sholmes went to bed in a very bad humour. Early next morning he received the following telephonic message:

"Arsène Lupin has the honour to inform you of his tragic death in the person of Monsieur Bresson, and requests the honour of your presence at the funeral service and burial, which will be held at public expense on Thursday, 25 June."

Chapter 8

THE SHIPWRECK

"THAT's what I don't like, Wilson," said Herlock Sholmes, after he had read Arsène Lupin's message; "that is what exasperates me in this affair—to feel that the cunning, mocking eye of that fellow follows me everywhere. He sees everything; he knows everything; he reads my inmost thoughts; he even foresees my slightest movement. Ah! He is possessed of a marvellous intuition, far surpassing that of the most instinctive woman, yes, surpassing even that of Herlock Sholmes himself. Nothing escapes him. I resemble an actor whose every step and movement are directed by a stage-manager; who says this and does that in obedience to a superior will. That is my position. Do you understand, Wilson?"

Certainly Wilson would have understood if his faculties had not been deadened by the profound slumber of a man whose temperature varies between one hundred and one hundred and three degrees. But whether he heard or not was a matter of no consequence to Herlock Sholmes, who continued:

"I have to concentrate all my energy and bring all my resources into action in order to make the slightest progress. And, fortunately for me, those petty annoyances are like so many pricks from a needle and serve only to stimulate me. As soon as the heat of the wound is appeased and the shock to my vanity has subsided I say to myself: 'Amuse yourself, my dear fellow, but remember that he who laughs last laughs best. Sooner or later you will betray yourself.' For you know, Wilson, it was Lupin himself, who, by his first dispatch and the observation that it suggested to little Henriette, disclosed to me the secret of his correspondence with Alice Hemun. Have you forgotten that circumstance, dear boy?"

But Wilson was asleep; and Sholmes, pacing to and fro, resumed his speech:

"And, now, things are not in a bad shape; a little obscure, perhaps, but the light is creeping in. In the first place, I must learn all about Monsieur Bresson. Ganimard and I will visit the bank of the river, at the spot where Bresson threw away the package, and the particular role of that gentleman will be known to me. After that the game will be played between me and Alice Demun. Rather a light-weight opponent, hein, Wilson? And do you not think that I will soon know the phrase represented by the letters clipped from the alphabet-book, and what the isolated letters—the 'C' and the 'H'—mean? That is all I want to know, Wilson."

Mademoiselle entered at that moment, and, observing Sholmes gesticulating, she said, in her sweetest manner:

"Monsieur Sholmes, I must scold you if you waken my patient. It isn't nice of you to disturb him. The doctor has ordered absolute rest."

He looked at her in silence, astonished, as on their first meeting, at her wonderful self-possession.

"Why do you look at me so, Monsieur Sholmes?... You seem to be trying to read my thoughts... No?... Then what is it?"

She questioned him with the most innocent expression on her pretty face and in her frank blue eyes. A smile played upon her lips; and she displayed so much unaffected candour that the Englishman almost lost his temper. He approached her and said, in a low voice:

"Bresson killed himself last night."

She affected not to understand him; so he repeated:

"Bresson killed himself yesterday..."

She did not show the slightest emotion; she acted as if the matter did not concern or interest her in any way.

"You have been informed," said Sholmes, displaying his annoyance. "Otherwise, the news would have caused you to start, at least. Ah! you are stronger than I expected. But what's the use of your trying to conceal anything from me?"

He picked up the alphabet-book, which he had placed on a convenient table, and, opening it at the mutilated page, said:

"Will you tell me the order in which the missing letters should be arranged in order to express the exact wording of the message you sent to Bresson four days before the theft of the Jewish lamp?"

"The order?... Bresson?... the theft of the Jewish lamp?"

She repeated the words slowly, as if trying to grasp their meaning. He continued:

"Yes. Here are the letters employed... on this bit of paper... What did you say to Bresson?"

"The letters employed... what did I say..."

Suddenly she burst into laughter:

"Ah! That is it! I understand! I am an accomplice in the crime! There is a Monsieur Bresson who stole the Jewish lamp and who has now committed suicide. And I am the friend of that gentleman. Oh! How absurd you are!"

"Whom did you go to see last night on the second floor of a house in the avenue des Ternes?"

"Who? My modiste, Mademoiselle Langeais. Do you suppose that my modiste and my friend Monsieur Bresson are the same person?"

Despite all he knew, Sholmes was now in doubt. A person can feign terror, joy, anxiety, in fact all emotions; but a person cannot feign absolute indifference or light, careless laughter. Yet he continued to question her:

"Why did you accost me the other evening at the Northern Railway station? And why did you entreat me to leave Paris immediately without investigating this theft?"

"Ah! you are too inquisitive, Monsieur Sholmes," she replied, still laughing in the most natural manner. "To punish you I will tell you nothing, and, besides, you must watch the patient while I go to the pharmacy on an urgent message. Au revoir."

She left the room.

"I am beaten... by a girl," muttered Sholmes. "Not only did I get nothing out of her but I exposed my hand and put her on her guard."

And he recalled the affair of the blue diamond and his first interview with Clotilde Destange. Had not the blonde Lady met his question with the same unruffled serenity, and was he not once more face to face with one of those creatures who, under the protection and influence of Arsène Lupin, maintain the utmost coolness in the face of a terrible danger?

"Sholmes... Sholmes..."

It was Wilson who called him. Sholmes approached the bed, and, leaning over, said:

"What's the matter, Wilson? Does your wound pain you?"

Wilson's lips moved, but he could not speak. At last, with a great effort, he stammered:

"No... Sholmes... it is not she... that is impossible——"

"Come, Wilson, what do you know about it? I tell you that it is she! It is only when I meet one of Lupin's creatures, prepared and instructed by him, that I lose my head and make a fool of myself... I bet you that within an hour Lupin will know all about our interview. Within an hour? What am I saying?... Why, he may know already. The visit to the pharmacy... urgent message. All nonsense!... She has gone to telephone to Lupin."

Sholmes left the house hurriedly, went down the avenue de Messine, and was just in time to see Mademoiselle enter a pharmacy. Ten minutes later she emerged from the shop carrying some small packages and a bottle wrapped in white paper. But she had not proceeded far, when she was accosted by a man who, with hat in hand and an obsequious air, appeared to be asking for charity. She stopped, gave him something, and proceeded on her way.

"She spoke to him," said the Englishman to himself.

If not a certainty, it was at least an intuition, and quite sufficient to cause him to change his tactics. Leaving the girl to pursue her own course, he followed the suspected mendicant, who walked slowly to the avenue des Ternes and lingered for a long time around the house in which Bresson had lived, sometimes raising his eyes to the windows of the second floor and watching the people who entered the house.

At the end of an hour he climbed to the top of a tramcar going in the direction of Neuilly. Sholmes followed and took a seat behind the man, and beside a gentleman who was concealed behind the pages of a newspaper. At the fortifications the gentleman lowered the paper, and Sholmes recognized Ganimard, who thereupon whispered, as he pointed to the man in front:

"It is the man who followed Bresson last night. He has been watching the house for an hour."

"Anything new in regard to Bresson?" asked Sholmes.

"Yes, a letter came to his address this morning."

"This morning? Then it was posted yesterday before the sender could know of Bresson's death."

"Exactly. It is now in the possession of the examining magistrate. But I read it. It says: *He will not accept any compromise. He wants everything—the first thing as well as those of the second affair. Otherwise he will proceed.*"

"There is no signature," added Ganimard. "It seems to me those few lines won't help us much."

"I don't agree with you, Monsieur Ganimard. To me those few lines are very interesting."

"Why so? I can't see it."

"For reasons that are personal to me," replied Sholmes, with the indifference that he frequently displayed toward his colleague.

The tramcar stopped at the rue de Château, which was the terminus. The man descended and walked away quietly. Sholmes followed at so short a distance that Ganimard protested, saying:

"If he should turn around he will suspect us."

"He will not turn around."

"How do you know?"

"He is an accomplice of Arsène Lupin, and the fact that he walks in that manner, with his hands in his pockets, proves, in the first place, that he knows he is being followed and, in the second place, that he is not afraid."

"But I think we are keeping too close to him."

"Not too close to prevent his slipping through our fingers. He is too sure of himself."

"Ah! Look there! In front of that café there are two of the bicycle police. If I summon them to our assistance, how can the man slip through our fingers?"

"Well, our friend doesn't seem to be worried about it. In fact, he is asking for their assistance himself."

"Mon Dieu!" exclaimed Ganimard, "he has a nerve."

The man approached the two policemen just as they were mounting their bicycles. After a few words with them he leaped on a third bicycle, which was leaning against the wall of the café, and rode away at a fast pace, accompanied by the two policemen.

"Hein! One, two, three and away!" growled Sholmes. "And through, whose agency, Monsieur Ganimard? Two of your colleagues... Ah! but Arsène Lupin has a wonderful organization! Bicycle policemen in his service!... I told you our man was too calm, too sure of himself."

"Well, then," said Ganimard, quite vexed, "what are we to do now? It is easy enough to laugh! Anyone can do that."

"Come, come, don't lose your temper! We will get our revenge. But, in the meantime, we need reinforcements."

"Folenfant is waiting for me at the end of the avenue de Neuilly."

"Well, go and get him and join me later. I will follow our fugitive."

Sholmes followed the bicycle tracks, which were plainly visible in the dust of the road as two of the machines were furnished with striated tires. Very soon he ascertained that the tracks were leading him to the edge of the Seine, and that the three men had turned in the direction taken by Bresson on the preceding evening. Thus he arrived at the gateway where he and Ganimard had concealed themselves, and, a little farther on, he discovered a mingling of the bicycle tracks which showed that the men had halted at that spot. Directly opposite there was a little point of land which projected into the river and, at the extremity thereof, an old boat was moored.

It was there that Bresson had thrown away the package, or, rather, had dropped it. Sholmes descended the bank and saw that the declivity was not steep and the water quite shallow, so it would be quite easy to recover the package, provided the three men had not forestalled him.

"No, that can't be," he thought, "they have not had time. A quarter of an hour at the most. And yet, why did they come this way?"

A fisherman was seated on the old boat. Sholmes asked him:

"Did you see three men on bicycles a few minutes ago?"

The fisherman made a negative gesture. But Sholmes insisted:

"Three men who stopped on the road just on top of the bank?"

The fisherman rested his pole under his arm, took a memorandum book from his pocket, wrote on one of the pages, tore it out, and handed it to Sholmes. The Englishman gave a start of surprise. In the middle of the paper which he held in his hand he saw the series of letters cut from the alphabet-book:

CDEHNOPRZEO—237.

The man resumed his fishing, sheltered from the sun by a large straw hat, with his coat and vest lying beside him. He was intently watching the cork attached to his line as it floated on the surface of the water.

There was a moment of silence—solemn and terrible.

"Is it he?" conjectured Sholmes, with an anxiety that was almost pitiful. Then the truth burst upon him:

"It is he! It is he! No one else could remain there so calmly, without the slightest display of anxiety, without the least fear of what might happen. And who else would know the story of those mysterious letters? Alice had warned him by means of her messenger."

Suddenly the Englishman felt that his hand—that his own hand had involuntarily seized the handle of his revolver, and that his eyes were fixed on the man's back, a little below the neck. One movement, and the drama would be finished; the life of the strange adventurer would come to a miserable end.

The fisherman did not stir.

Sholmes nervously toyed with his revolver, and experienced a wild desire to fire it and end everything; but the horror of such an act was repugnant to his nature. Death would be certain and would end all.

"Ah!" he thought, "let him get up and defend himself. If he doesn't, so much the worse for him. One second more... and I fire..."

But a sound of footsteps behind him caused him to turn his head. It was Ganimard coming with some assistants.

Then, quickly changing his plans, Sholmes leaped into the boat, which was broken from its moorings by his sudden action; he pounced upon the man and seized him around the body. They rolled to the bottom of the boat together.

"Well, now!" exclaimed Lupin, struggling to free himself, "what does this mean? When one of us has conquered the other, what good will it do? You will not know what to do with me, nor I with you. We will remain here like two idiots."

The two oars slipped into the water. The boat drifted into the stream.

"Good Lord, what a fuss you make! A man of your age ought to know better! You act like a child."

Lupin succeeded in freeing himself from the grasp of the detective, who, thoroughly exasperated and ready to kill, put his hand in his pocket. He uttered an oath: Lupin had taken his revolver. Then he knelt down and tried to capture one of the lost oars in order to regain the shore, while Lupin was trying to capture the other oar in order to drive the boat down the river.

"It's gone! I can't reach it," said Lupin. "But it's of no consequence. If you get your oar I can prevent your using it. And you could do the same to me. But, you see, that is the way in this world, we act without any purpose or reason, as our efforts are in vain since Fate decides everything. Now, don't you see, Fate is on the side of his friend Lupin. The game is mine! The current favours me!"

The boat was slowly drifting down the river.

"Look out!" cried Lupin, quickly.

Someone on the bank was pointing a revolver. Lupin stooped, a shot was fired; it struck the water beyond the boat. Lupin burst into laughter.

"God bless me! It's my friend Ganimard! But it was very wrong of you to do that, Ganimard. You have no right to shoot except in self-defence. Does poor Lupin worry you so much that you forget yourself?... Now, be good, and don't shoot again!... If you do you will hit our English friend."

He stood behind Sholmes, facing Ganimard, and said:

"Now, Ganimard, I am ready! Aim for his heart!... Higher!... A little to the left... Ah! You missed that time ... deuced bad shot... Try again... Your hand shakes, Ganimard... Now, once more ... one, two, three, fire!... Missed!... Parbleu! the authorities furnish you with toy-pistols."

Lupin drew a long revolver and fired without taking aim. Ganimard put his hand to his hat: the bullet had passed through it.

"What do you think of that, Ganimard! Ah! That's a real revolver! A genuine English bulldog. It belongs to my friend, Herlock Sholmes."

And, with a laugh, he threw the revolver to the shore, where it landed at Ganimard's feet.

Sholmes could not withhold a smile of admiration. What a torrent of youthful spirits! And how he seemed to enjoy himself! It appeared as if the sensation of peril caused him a physical pleasure; and this extraordinary man had no other purpose in life than to seek for dangers simply for the amusement it afforded him in avoiding them.

Many people had now gathered on the banks of the river, and Ganimard and his men followed the boat as it slowly floated down the stream. Lupin's capture was a mathematical certainty.

"Confess, old fellow," said Lupin, turning to the Englishman, "that you would not exchange your present position for all the gold in the Transvaal! You are now in the first row of the orchestra chairs! But, in the first place, we must have the prologue... after which we can leap, at one bound, to the fifth act of the drama, which will represent the capture or escape of Arsène Lupin. Therefore, I am going to ask you a plain question, to which I request a plain answer—a simple yes or no. Will you renounce this affair? At present I can repair the damage you have done; later it will be beyond my power. Is it a bargain?"

"No."

Lupin's face showed his disappointment and annoyance. He continued:

"I insist. More for your sake than my own, I insist, because I am certain you will be the first to regret your intervention. For the last time, yes or no?"

"No."

Lupin stooped down, removed one of the boards in the bottom of the boat, and, for some minutes, was engaged in a work the nature of which Sholmes could not discern. Then he arose, seated himself beside the Englishman, and said:

"I believe, monsieur, that we came to the river today for the same purpose: to recover the object which Bresson threw away. For my part I had invited a few friends to join me here, and I was on the point of making an examination of the bed of the river when my friends announced your approach. I confess that the news did not surprise me, as I have been notified every hour concerning the progress of your investigation. That was an easy matter. Whenever anything occurred in the rue Murillo that might interest me, simply a ring on the telephone and I was informed."

He stopped. The board that he had displaced in the bottom of the boat was rising and water was working into the boat all around it.

"The deuce! I didn't know how to fix it. I was afraid this old boat would leak. You are not afraid, monsieur?"

Sholmes shrugged his shoulders. Lupin continued:

"You will understand then, in those circumstances, and knowing in advance that you would be more eager to seek a battle than I would be to avoid it, I assure you I was not entirely displeased to enter into a contest of which the issue is quite certain, since I hold all the trump cards in my hand. And I desired that our meeting should be given the widest publicity in order that your defeat may be universally known, so that another Countess de Crozon or another Baron d'Imblevalle may not be tempted to solicit your aid against me. Besides, my dear monsieur—"

He stopped again and, using his half-closed hands as a lorgnette, he scanned the banks of the river.

"Mon Dieu! they have chartered a superb boat, a real war-vessel, and see how they are rowing. In five minutes they will be along-side, and I am lost. Monsieur Sholmes, a word of advice; you seize me, bind me and deliver me to the officers of the law. Does that programme please you?... Unless, in the meantime, we are shipwrecked, in which event we can do nothing but prepare our wills. What do you think?"

They exchanged looks. Sholmes now understood Lupin's scheme: he had scuttled the boat. And the water was rising. It had reached the soles of their boots. Then it covered their feet; but they did not move. It was half-way to their knees. The Englishman took out his tobacco, rolled a cigarette, and lighted it. Lupin continued to talk:

"But do not regard that offer as a confession of my weakness. I surrender to you in a battle in which I can achieve a victory in order to avoid a struggle upon a field not of my own choosing. In so doing I recognize the fact that Sholmes is the only enemy I fear, and announce my anxiety that Sholmes will not be diverted from my track. I take this opportunity to tell you these things since fate has accorded me the honour of a conversation with you. I have only one regret; it is that our conversation should have occurred while we are taking a foot-bath... a situation that is lacking in dignity, I must confess... What did I say? A foot-bath? It is worse than that."

The water had reached the board on which they were sitting, and the boat was gradually sinking.

Sholmes, smoking his cigarette, appeared to be calmly admiring the scenery. For nothing in the world, while face to face with that man who, while threatened by dangers, surrounded by a crowd, followed by a posse of police, maintained his equanimity and good humour, for nothing in the world would he, Sholmes, display the slightest sign of nervousness.

Each of them looked as if he might say: Should a person be disturbed by such trifles? Are not people drowned in a river every day? Is it such an unusual event as to deserve special attention? One chatted, whilst the other dreamed; both concealing their wounded pride beneath a mask of indifference.

One minute more and the boat will sink. Lupin continued his chatter:

"The important thing to know is whether we will sink before or after the arrival of the champions of the law. That is the main question. As to our shipwreck, that is a foregone conclusion. Now, monsieur, the hour has come in which we must make our wills. I give, devise and bequeath all my property to Herlock Sholmes, a citizen of England, for his own use and benefit. But, mon Dieu, how quickly the champions of the law are approaching! Ah! the brave fellows! It is a pleasure to watch them. Observe the precision of the oars! Ah! is it you, Brigadier Folenfant? Bravo! The idea of a war-vessel is an excellent one. I commend you to your superiors, Brigadier Folenfant... Do you wish a medal? You shall have it. And your comrade Dieuzy, where is he?... Ah! yes, I think I see him on the left bank of the river at the head of a hundred natives. So that, if I escape shipwreck, I shall be captured on the left by Dieuzy and his natives, or, on the right, by Ganimard and the populace of Neuilly. An embarrassing dilemma!"

The boat entered an eddy; it swung around and Sholmes caught hold of the oarlocks. Lupin said to him:

"Monsieur, you should remove your coat. You will find it easier to swim without a coat. No? You refuse? Then I shall put on my own."

He donned his coat, buttoned it closely, the same as Sholmes, and said:

"What a discourteous man you are! And what a pity that you should be so stubborn in this affair, in which, of course, you display your strength, but, oh! So vainly! Really, you mar your genius—"

"Monsieur Lupin," interrupted Sholmes, emerging from his silence, "you talk too much, and you frequently err through excess of confidence and through your frivolity."

"That is a severe reproach."

"Thus, without knowing it, you furnished me, only a moment ago, with the information I required."

"What! you required some information and you didn't tell me?"

"I had no occasion to ask you for it—you volunteered it. Within three hours I can deliver the key of the mystery to Monsieur d'Imblevalle. That is the only reply—"

He did not finish the sentence. The boat suddenly sank, taking both of the men down with it. It emerged immediately, with its keel in the air. Shouts were heard on either bank, succeeded by an anxious moment of silence. Then the shouts were renewed: one of the shipwrecked party had come to the surface.

It was Herlock Sholmes. He was an excellent swimmer, and struck out, with powerful strokes, for Folenfant's boat.

"Courage, Monsieur Sholmes," shouted Folenfant; "we are here. Keep it up... we will get you... a little more, Monsieur Sholmes... catch the rope."

The Englishman seized the rope they had thrown to him. But, while they were hauling him into the boat, he heard a voice behind him, saying:

"The key of the mystery, monsieur, yes, you shall have it. I am astonished that you haven't got it already. What then? What good will it do you? By that time you will have lost the battle..."

Now comfortably installed astride the keel of the boat, Lupin continued his speech with solemn gestures, as if he hoped to convince his adversary.

"You must understand, my dear Sholmes, there is nothing to be done, absolutely nothing. You find yourself in the deplorable position of a gentleman—"

"Surrender, Lupin!" shouted Folenfant.

"You are an ill-bred fellow, Folenfant, to interrupt me in the middle of a sentence. I was saying—"

"Surrender, Lupin!"

"Oh! Parbleu! Brigadier Folenfant, a man surrenders only when he is in danger. Surely, you do not pretend to say that I am in any danger."

"For the last time, Lupin, I call on you to surrender."

"Brigadier Folenfant, you have no intention of killing me; you may wish to wound me since you are afraid I may escape. But if by chance the wound prove mortal! Just think of your remorse! It would embitter your old age."

The shot was fired.

Lupin staggered, clutched at the keel of the boat for a moment, then let go and disappeared.

It was exactly three o'clock when the foregoing events transpired. Precisely at six o'clock, as he had foretold, Herlock Sholmes, dressed in trousers that were too short and a coat that was too small, which he had borrowed from an innkeeper at Neuilly, wearing a cap and a flannel shirt, entered the boudoir in the Rue Murillo, after having sent word to Monsieur and Madame d'Imblevalle that he desired an interview.

They found him walking up and down the room. And he looked so ludicrous in his strange costume that they could scarcely suppress their mirth. With pensive air and stooped shoulders, he walked like an automaton from the window to the door and from the door to the window, taking each time the same number of steps, and turning each time in the same manner.

He stopped, picked up a small ornament, examined it mechanically, and resumed his walk. At last, planting himself before them, he asked:

"Is Mademoiselle here?"

"Yes, she is in the garden with the children."'

"I wish Mademoiselle to be present at this interview."

"Is it necessary—"

"Have a little patience, monsieur. From the facts I am going to present to you, you will see the necessity for her presence here."

"Very well. Suzanne, will you call her?"

Madame d'Imblevalle arose, went out, and returned almost immediately, accompanied by Alice Demun. Mademoiselle, who was a trifle paler than usual, remained standing, leaning against a table, and without even asking why she had been called. Sholmes did not look at her, but, suddenly turning toward Monsieur d'Imblevalle, he said, in a tone which did not admit of a reply:

"After several days' investigation, monsieur, I must repeat what I told you when I first came here: the Jewish lamp was stolen by someone living in the house."

"The name of the guilty party?"

"I know it."

"Your proof?"

"I have sufficient to establish that fact."

"But we require more than that. We desire the restoration of the stolen goods."

"The Jewish lamp? It is in my possession."

"The opal necklace? The snuff-box?"

"The opal necklace, the snuff-box, and all the goods stolen on the second occasion are in my possession."

Sholmes delighted in these dramatic dialogues, and it pleased him to announce his victories in that curt manner. The baron and his wife were amazed, and looked at Sholmes with a silent curiosity, which was the highest praise.

He related to them, very minutely, what he had done during those three days. He told of his discovery of the alphabet book, wrote upon a sheet of paper the sentence formed by the missing letters, then related the journey of Bresson to the bank of the river and the suicide of the adventurer, and, finally, his struggle with Lupin, the shipwreck, and the disappearance of Lupin. When he had finished, the baron said, in a low voice:

"Now, you have told us everything except the name of the guilty party. Whom do you accuse?"

"I accuse the person who cut the letters from the alphabet book, and communicated with Arsène Lupin by means of those letters."

"How do you know that such correspondence was carried on with Arsène Lupin?"

"My information comes from Lupin himself."

He produced a piece of paper that was wet and crumpled. It was the page which Lupin had torn from his memorandum-book, and upon which he had written the phrase.

"And you will notice," said Sholmes, with satisfaction, "that he was not obliged to give me that sheet of paper, and, in that way, disclose his identity. Simple childishness on his part, and yet it gave me exactly the information I desired."

"What was it?" asked the baron. "I don't understand."

Sholmes took a pencil and made a fresh copy of the letters and figures.

"CDEHNOPRZEO—237."

"Well?" said the baron; "it is the formula you showed me yourself."

"No. If you had turned and returned that formula in every way, as I have done, you would have seen at first glance that this formula is not like the first one."

"In what respect do they differ?"

"This one has two more letters—an E and an O."

"Really; I hadn't noticed that."

"Join those two letters to the C and the H which remained after forming the word 'respondez,' and you will agree with me that the only possible word is ECHO."

"What does that mean?"

"It refers to the *Echo de France*, Lupin's newspaper, his official organ, the one in which he publishes his communications. Reply in the *Echo de France*, in the personal advertisements, under number 237. That is the key to the mystery, and Arsène Lupin was kind enough to furnish it to me. I went to the newspaper office."

"What did you find there?"

"I found the entire story of the relations between Arsène Lupin and his accomplice."

Sholmes produced seven newspapers which he opened at the fourth page and pointed to the following lines:

1. Ars. Lup. Lady implores protection. 540.

2. 540. Awaiting particulars. A.L.

3. A.L. Under domin. enemy. Lost.

4. 540. Write address. Will make investigation.

5. A.L. Murillo.

6. 540. Park three o'clock. Violets.

7. 237. Understand. Sat. Will be Sun. morn. park.

"And you call that the whole story!" exclaimed the baron.

"Yes, and if you will listen to me for a few minutes, I think I can convince you. In the first place, a lady who signs herself 540 implores the protection of Arsène Lupin, who replies by asking for particulars. The lady replies that she is under the domination of an enemy—who is Bresson, no doubt—and that she is lost if someone does not come to her assistance. Lupin is suspicious and does not yet venture to appoint an interview with the unknown woman, demands the address and proposes to make an investigation. The lady hesitates for four days—look at the dates—finally, under stress of circumstances and influenced by Bresson's threats, she gives the name of the street—Murillo. Next day, Arsène Lupin announces that he will be in the Park Monceau at three o'clock, and asks his unknown correspondent to wear a bouquet of violets as a means of identification. Then there is a lapse of eight days in the correspondence. Arsène Lupin and the lady do not require to correspond through the newspaper now, as they see each other or write directly. The scheme is arranged in this way: in order to satisfy Bresson's demands, the lady is to carry off the Jewish lamp. The date is not yet fixed. The lady who, as a matter of prudence, corresponds by means of letters cut out of a book, decides on Saturday and adds: *Reply Echo 237*. Lupin replies that it is understood and that he will be in the park on Sunday morning. Sunday morning, the theft takes place."

"Really, that is an excellent chain of circumstantial evidence and every link is complete," said the baron.

"The theft has taken place," continued Sholmes. "The lady goes out on Sunday morning, tells Lupin what she has done, and carries the Jewish lamp to Bresson. Everything occurs then exactly as Lupin had foreseen. The officers of the law, deceived by an open window, four holes in the ground and two scratches on the balcony railing, immediately advance the theory that the theft was committed by a burglar. The lady is safe."

"Yes, I confess the theory was a logical one," said the baron. "But the second theft—"

"The second theft was provoked by the first. The newspapers having related how the Jewish lamp had disappeared, someone conceived the idea of repeating the crime and carrying away what had been left. This time, it was not a simulated theft, but a real one, a genuine burglary, with ladders and other paraphernalia—"

"Lupin, of course—"

"No. Lupin does not act so stupidly. He doesn't fire at people for trifling reasons."

"Then, who was it?"

"Bresson, no doubt, and unknown to the lady whom he had menaced. It was Bresson who entered here; it was Bresson that I pursued; it was Bresson who wounded poor Wilson."

"Are you sure of it?"

"Absolutely. One of Bresson's accomplices wrote to him yesterday, before his suicide, a letter which proves that negotiations were pending between this accomplice and Lupin for the restitution of all the articles stolen from your house. Lupin demanded everything, '*the first thing* (that is, the Jewish lamp) *as well as those of the second affair.*' Moreover, he was watching Bresson. When the latter returned from the river last night, one of Lupin's men followed him as well as we."

"What was Bresson doing at the river?"

"Having been warned of the progress of my investigations—"

"Warned! By whom?"

"By the same lady, who justly feared that the discovery of the Jewish lamp would lead to the discovery of her own adventure. Thereupon, Bresson, having been warned, made into a package all the things that could compromise him and threw them into a place where he thought he could get them again when the danger was past. It was after his return, tracked by Ganimard and myself, having, no doubt, other sins on his conscience, that he lost his head and killed himself."

"But what did the package contain?"

"The Jewish lamp and your other ornaments."

"Then, they are not in your possession?"

"Immediately after Lupin's disappearance, I profited by the bath he had forced upon me, went to the spot selected by Bresson, where I found the stolen articles wrapped in some soiled linen. They are there, on the table."

Without a word, the baron cut the cord, tore open the wet linen, picked out the lamp, turned a screw in the foot, then divided the bowl of the lamp which opened in two equal parts and there he found the golden chimera, set with rubies and emeralds.

It was intact.

There was in that scene, so natural in appearance and which consisted of a simple exposition of facts, something which rendered it frightfully tragic—it was the formal, direct, irrefutable accusation that Sholmes launched in each of his words against Mademoiselle. And it was also the impressive silence of Alice Demun.

During that long, cruel accumulation of accusing circumstances heaped one upon another, not a muscle of her face had moved, not a trace of revolt or fear had marred the serenity of her limpid eyes. What were her thoughts. And, especially, what was she going to say at the solemn moment when it would become necessary for her to speak and defend herself in order to break the chain of evidence that Herlock Sholmes had so cleverly woven around her?

That moment had come, but the girl was silent.

"Speak! Speak!" cried Mon. d'Imblevalle.

She did not speak. So he insisted:

"One word will clear you. One word of denial, and I will believe you."

That word, she would not utter.

The baron paced to and fro in his excitement; then, addressing Sholmes, he said:

"No, monsieur, I cannot believe it, I 9do not believe it. There are impossible crimes! And this is opposed to all I know and to all that I have seen during the past year. No, I cannot believe it."

He placed his hand on the Englishman's shoulder, and said:

"But you yourself, monsieur, are you absolutely certain that you are right?"

Sholmes hesitated, like a man on whom a sudden demand is made and cannot frame an immediate reply. Then he smiled, and said:

"Only the person whom I accuse, by reason of her situation in your house, could know that the Jewish lamp contained that magnificent jewel."

"I cannot believe it," repeated the baron.

"Ask her."

It was, really, the very thing he would not have done, blinded by the confidence the girl had inspired in him. But he could no longer refrain from doing it. He approached her and, looking into her eyes, said:

"Was it you, mademoiselle? Was it you who took the jewel? Was it you who corresponded with Arsène Lupin and committed the theft?"

"It was I, monsieur," she replied.

She did not drop her head. Her face displayed no sign of shame or fear.

"Is it possible?" murmured Mon. d'Imblevalle. "I would never have believed it... You are the last person in the world that I would have suspected. How did you do it?"

"I did it exactly as Monsieur Sholmes has told it. On Saturday night I came to the boudoir, took the lamp, and, in the morning I carried it... to that man."

"No," said the baron; "what you pretend to have done is impossible."

"Impossible—why?"

"Because, in the morning I found the door of the boudoir bolted."

She blushed, and looked at Sholmes as if seeking his counsel. Sholmes was astonished at her embarrassment. Had she nothing to say? Did the confessions, which had corroborated the report that he, Sholmes, had made concerning the theft of the Jewish lamp, merely serve to mask a lie? Was she misleading them by a false confession?

The baron continued:

"That door was locked. I found the door exactly as I had left it the night before. If you entered by that door, as you pretend, someone must have opened it from the interior—that is to say, from the boudoir or from our chamber. Now, there was no one inside these two rooms... there was no one except my wife and myself."

Sholmes bowed his head and covered his face with his hands in order to conceal his emotion. A sudden light had entered his mind, that startled him and made him exceedingly uncomfortable. Everything was revealed to him, like the sudden lifting of a fog from the morning landscape. He was annoyed as well as ashamed, because his deductions were fallacious and his entire theory was wrong.

Alice Demun was innocent!

Alice Demun was innocent. That proposition explained the embarrassment he had experienced from the beginning in directing the terrible accusation against that young girl. Now, he saw the truth; he knew it. After a few seconds, he raised his head, and looked at Madame d'Imblevalle as naturally as he could. She was pale—with that unusual pallor which invades us in the relentless moments of our lives. Her hands, which she endeavoured to conceal, were trembling as if stricken with palsy.

"One minute more," thought Sholmes, "and she will betray herself."

He placed himself between her and her husband in the desire to avert the awful danger which, *through his fault*, now threatened that man and woman. But, at sight of the baron, he was shocked to the very centre of his soul. The same dreadful idea had entered the mind of Monsieur d'Imblevalle. The same thought was at work in the brain of the husband. He understood, also! He saw the truth!

In desperation, Alice Demun hurled herself against the implacable truth, saying:

"You are right, monsieur. I made a mistake. I did not enter by this door. I came through the garden and the vestibule =... by aid of a ladder—"

It was a supreme effort of true devotion. But a useless effort! The words rang false. The voice did not carry conviction, and the poor girl no longer displayed those clear, fearless eyes and that natural air of innocence which had served her so well. Now, she bowed her head—vanquished.

The silence became painful. Madame d'Imblevalle was waiting for her husband's next move, overwhelmed with anxiety and fear. The baron appeared to be struggling against the dreadful suspicion, as if he would not submit to the overthrow of his happiness. Finally, he said to his wife:

"Speak! Explain!"

"I have nothing to tell you," she replied, in a very low voice, and with features drawn by anguish.

"So, then... Mademoiselle..."

"Mademoiselle saved me... through devotion... through affection... and accused herself..."

"Saved you from what? From whom?"

"From that man."

"Bresson?"

"Yes; it was I whom he held in fear by threats... I met him at one of my friends'... and I was foolish enough to listen to him. Oh! There was nothing that you cannot pardon. But I wrote him two letters... letters which you will see... I had to buy them back ... you know how... Oh! have pity on me?... I have suffered so much!"

"You! You! Suzanne!"

He raised his clenched fists, ready to strike her, ready to kill her. But he dropped his arms, and murmured:

"You, Suzanne... You!... Is it possible?"

By short detached sentences, she related the heartrending story, her dreadful awakening to the infamy of the man, her remorse, her fear, and she also told of Alice's devotion; how the young girl divined the sorrow of her mistress, wormed a confession out of her, wrote to Lupin, and devised the scheme of the theft in order to save her from Bresson.

"You, Suzanne, you," repeated Monsieur d'Imblevalle, bowed with grief and shame... "How could you?"

* * *

On the same evening, the steamer "City of London," which plies between Calais and Dover, was gliding slowly over the smooth sea. The night was dark; the wind was fainter than a zephyr. The majority of the passengers had retired to their cabins; but a few, more intrepid, were promenading on the deck or sleeping in large rocking-chairs, wrapped in their travelling-rugs. One could see, here and there, the light of a cigar, and one could hear, mingled with the soft murmur of the breeze, the faint sound of voices which were carefully subdued to harmonize with the deep silence of the night.

One of the passengers, who had been pacing to and fro upon the deck, stopped before a woman who was lying on a bench, scrutinized her, and, when she moved a little, he said:

"I thought you were asleep, Mademoiselle Alice."

"No, Monsieur Sholmes, I am not sleepy. I was thinking."

"Of what? If I may be so bold as to inquire?"

"I was thinking of Madame d'Imblevalle. She must be very unhappy. Her life is ruined."

"Oh! no, no," he replied quickly. "Her mistake was not a serious one. Monsieur d'Imblevalle will forgive and forget it. Why, even before we left, his manner toward her had softened."

"Perhaps ... but he will remember it for a long time ... and she will suffer a great deal."

"You love her?"

"Very much. It was my love for her that gave me strength to smile when I was trembling from fear, that gave me courage to look in your face when I desired to hide from your sight."

"And you are sorry to leave her?"

"Yes, very sorry. I have no relatives, no friends—but her."

"You will have friends," said the Englishman, who was affected by her sorrow. "I have promised that. I have relatives ... and some influence. I assure you that you will have no cause to regret coming to England."

"That may be, monsieur, but Madame d'Imblevalle will not be there."

Herlock Sholmes resumed his promenade upon the deck. After a few minutes, he took a seat near his travelling companion, filled his pipe, and struck four matches in a vain effort to light it. Then, as he had no more matches, he arose and said to a gentleman who was sitting near him:

"May I trouble you for a match?"

The gentleman opened a box of matches and struck one. The flame lighted up his face. Sholmes recognized him—it was Arsène Lupin.

If the Englishman had not given an almost imperceptible movement of surprise, Lupin would have supposed that his presence on board had been known to Sholmes, so well did he control his feelings and so natural was the easy manner in which he extended his hand to his adversary.

"How's the good health, Monsieur Lupin?"

"Bravo!" exclaimed Lupin, who could not repress a cry of admiration at the Englishman's sang-froid.

"Bravo? and why?"

"Why? Because I appear before you like a ghost, only a few hours after you saw me drowned in the Seine; and through pride—a quality that is essentially English—you evince not the slightest surprise. You greet me as a matter of course. Ah! I repeat: Bravo! Admirable!"

"There is nothing remarkable about it. From the manner in which you fell from the boat, I knew very well that you fell voluntarily, and that the bullet had not touched you."

"And you went away without knowing what had become of me?"

"What had become of you? Why, I knew that. There were at least five hundred people on the two banks of the river within a space of half-a-mile. If you escaped death, your capture was certain."

"And yet I am here."

"Monsieur Lupin, there are two men in the world at whom I am never astonished: in the first place, myself—and then, Arsène Lupin."

The treaty of peace was concluded.

If Sholmes had not been successful in his contests with Arsène Lupin; if Lupin remained the only enemy whose capture he must never hope to accomplish; if, in the course of their struggles, he had not always displayed a superiority, the Englishman had, none the less, by means of his extraordinary intuition and tenacity, succeeded in recovering the Jewish lamp as well as the blue diamond.

This time, perhaps, the finish had not been so brilliant, especially from the stand-point of the public spectators, since Sholmes was obliged to maintain a discreet silence in regard to the circumstances in which the Jewish lamp had been recovered, and to announce that he did not know the name of the thief. But as man to man, Arsène Lupin against Herlock Sholmes, detective against burglar, there was neither victor nor vanquished. Each of them had won corresponding victories.

Therefore they could now converse as courteous adversaries who had lain down their arms and held each other in high regard.

At Sholmes' request, Arsène Lupin related the strange story of his escape.

"If I may dignify it by calling it an escape," he said. "It was so simple! My friends were watching for me, as I had asked them to meet me there to recover the Jewish lamp. So, after remaining a good half-hour under the overturned boat, I took advantage of an occasion when Folenfant and his men were searching for my dead body along the bank of the river, to climb on top of the boat. Then my friends simply picked me up as they passed by in their motor-boat, and we sailed away under the staring eyes of an astonished multitude, including Ganimard and Folenfant."

"Very good," exclaimed Sholmes, "very neatly played. And now you have some business in England?"

"Yes, some accounts to square up... But I forgot ... what about Monsieur d'Imblevalle?"

"He knows everything."

"All! my dear Sholmes, what did I tell you? The wrong is now irreparable. Would it not have been better to have allowed me to carry out the affair in my own way? In a day or two more, I should have recovered the stolen goods from Bresson, restored them to Monsieur d'Imblevalle, and those two honest citizens would have lived together in peace and happiness ever after. Instead of that—"

"Instead of that," said Sholmes, sneeringly, "I have mixed the cards and sown the seeds of discord in the bosom of a family that was under your protection."

"Mon Dieu! of course, I was protecting them. Must a person steal, cheat and wrong all the time?"

"Then you do good, also?"

"When I have the time. Besides, I find it amusing. Now, for instance, in our last adventure, I found it extremely diverting that I should be the good genius seeking to help and save unfortunate mortals, while you were the evil genius who dispensed only despair and tears."

"Tears! Tears!" protested Sholmes.

"Certainly! The d'Imblevalle household is demolished, and Alice Demun weeps."

"She could not remain any longer. Ganimard would have discovered her some day, and, through her, reached Madame d'Imblevalle."

"Quite right, monsieur; but whose fault is it?"

Two men passed by. Sholmes said to Lupin, in a friendly tone:

"Do you know those gentlemen?"

"I thought I recognized one of them as the captain of the steamer."

"And the other?"

"I don't know."

"It is Austin Gilett, who occupies in London a position similar to that of Monsieur Dudouis in Paris."

"Ah! how fortunate! Will you be so kind as to introduce me? Monsieur Dudouis is one of my best friends, and I shall be delighted to say as much of Monsieur Austin Gilett."

The two gentlemen passed again.

"And if I should take you at your word, Monsieur Lupin?" said Sholmes, rising, and seizing Lupin's wrist with a hand of iron.

"Why do you grasp me so tightly, monsieur? I am quite willing to follow you."

In fact, he allowed himself to be dragged along without the least resistance. The two gentlemen were disappearing from sight. Sholmes quickened his pace. His finger-nails even sank into Lupin's flesh.

"Come! Come!" he exclaimed, with a sort of feverish haste, in harmony with his action. "Come! quicker than that."

But he stopped suddenly. Alice Demun was following them.

"What are you doing, Mademoiselle? You need not come. You must not come!"

It was Lupin who replied:

"You will notice, monsieur, that she is not coming of her own free will. I am holding her wrist in the same tight grasp that you have on mine."

"Why!"

"Because I wish to present her also. Her part in the affair of the Jewish lamp is much more important than mine. Accomplice of Arsène Lupin, accomplice of Bresson, she has a right to tell her adventure with the Baroness d'Imblevalle—which will deeply interest Monsieur Gilett as an officer of the law. And by introducing her also, you will have carried your gracious intervention to the very limit, my dear Sholmes."

The Englishman released his hold on his prisoner's wrist. Lupin liberated Mademoiselle.

They stood looking at each other for a few seconds, silently and motionless. Then Sholmes returned to the bench and sat down, followed by Lupin and the girl. After a long silence, Lupin said: "You see, monsieur, whatever we may do, we will never be on the same side. You are on one side of the fence; I am on the other. We can exchange greetings, shake hands, converse a moment, but the fence is always there. You will remain Herlock Sholmes, detective, and I, Arsène Lupin, gentleman-burglar. And Herlock Sholmes will ever obey, more or less spontaneously, with more or less propriety, his instinct as a detective, which is to pursue the burglar and run him down, if possible. And Arsène Lupin, in obedience to his burglarious instinct, will always be occupied in avoiding the reach of the detective, and making sport of the detective, if he can do it. And, this time, he can do it. Ha-ha-ha!"

He burst into a loud laugh, cunning, cruel and odious.

Then, suddenly becoming serious, he addressed Alice Demun:

"You may be sure, mademoiselle, even when reduced to the last extremity, I shall not betray you. Arsène Lupin never betrays anyone—especially those whom he loves and admires. And, may I be permitted to say, I love and admire the brave, dear woman you have proved yourself to be."

He took from his pocket a visiting card, tore it in two, gave one-half of it to the girl, as he said, in a voice shaken with emotion:

"If Monsieur Sholmes' plans for you do not succeed, mademoiselle, go to Lady Strongborough—you can easily find her address—and give her that half of the card, and, at the same time, say to her: *Faithful friend*. Lady Strongborough will show you the true devotion of a sister."

"Thank you," said the girl; "I shall see her to-morrow."

"And now, Monsieur Sholmes," exclaimed Lupin, with the satisfied air of a gentleman who has fulfilled his duty, "I will say good-night. We will not land for an hour yet, so I will get that much rest."

He lay down on the bench, with his hands beneath his head.

In a short time the high cliffs of the English coast loomed up in the increasing light of a new-born day. The passengers emerged from the cabins and crowded the deck, eagerly gazing on the approaching shore. Austin Gilette passed by, accompanied by two men whom Sholmes recognized as sleuths from Scotland Yard.

Lupin was asleep, on his bench.

THE END